Leela Gour Broome enjoys playing with words—painting her puns into cartoons or cooking up real and imaginary yarns for children and anyone else who is willing to listen. She studied Western music and loves nature having experienced much of it first-hand in nine years of tea plantation life in South India. She thinks she is creative at craft, which she enjoys with her granddaughter. For sixteen glorious years she conducted nature and environment camps for kids she considers all her campers a part of her own family and from all accounts its a feeling that's apparently mutual. She collects quirky, decorative cows and has them all over her farmhouse. She is married to a diehard gentleman farmer and lives on an organic, wooded farm outside Pune, with a menagerie of pets, resident and migratory birds and some wild animals. To know more about the author and her experiences in the forest of southern India, visit her blog *www. fluteintheforest.blogspot.com*.

OTHER RUSKIN BOND RECOMMENDS PUFFIN TITLES

The Magic Store of Nu-Cham-Vu
Shreekumar Varma.

'Shreekumar Varma excels in tales of fantastic adventure in strange lands, and the toy shop of the horrible Nu-Cham-Vu provides plenty of scope for wondrous tales within tales in an exotic setting. Never a dull moment!'

Panna
Kamala Das

'A famous poet gives us a lovely story of fairy tale magic set along the sea coast near her home in Kerala. Just right for reading aloud to your children, or starting them off as readers in their own right. Kids will love the Fish King and Fish Queen, and little Panna will steal your heart.'

FLUTE IN THE FOREST

LEELA GOUR BROOME

Illustrations by
Ajanta Guhathakurta

PUFFIN BOOKS
An imprint of Penguin Random House

PUFFIN BOOKS

USA | Canada | UK | Ireland | Australia
New Zealand | India | South Africa | China | Singapore

Puffin Books is part of the Penguin Random House group of companies
whose addresses can be found at global.penguinrandomhouse.com

Published by Penguin Random House India Pvt. Ltd
4th Floor, Capital Tower 1, MG Road,
Gurugram 122 002, Haryana, India

Penguin
Random House
India

First published in Puffin by Penguin Books India 2010

Text copyright © Leela Gour Broome 2010
Illustrations copyright © Penguin Books India 2010
Illustrations by Ajanta Guhathakurta

10 9 8 7 6 5 4 3 2

ISBN 9780143331605

Typeset in Perpetua by InoSoft Systems
Printed at Manipal Technologies Limited, India

www.penguin.co.in

MIX
Paper | Supporting
responsible forestry
FSC® C043100

This is a legitimate digitally printed version of the book and therefore might not
have certain extra finishing on the cover.

For my granddaughter Aranya Pathak Broome.

A growing bond, happy times and green memories.

CONTENTS

ACKNOWLEDGEMENTS

I owe sincere thanks to my daughter Shonali, for the seed of an idea that got this book started. To my daughter-in-law Neema, for encouraging me right through. To my son Vivek, for helping me with memory sticks and thousands of Xerox copies. To my dear, patient husband Ashok, whose quiet listening during chapters that were read and reread helped to keep up the momentum till the final words were done.

So many Nature Trails Instructors, well-wishers and my young campers who were interested in this book. Mridula Vijairaghavan—who read the first manuscript, Sameer Joshi, Shilpa Agashe, Ashok Captain, Sharmila Deo, Bhagyashree and Bhakti Patwardhan, Lakshika Pandey, Devika Nadig and Vijay Gupta. Also to many more who would be impossible to name here, but without whose egging on, this book may never have got written—many thanks.

To long time friends from our tea-estate days—Muthu and Dalu Achaiah, Joe and Hermie Mathias, CMR and

Prema Daniel—thanks for great experiences that form the background of this book; to Kiran Chhokar who saw the writer in me when I was still a teenager, Nileem Shankar and Vera Irani who never stopped with their positive push! And to my sisters, Mohra Gavankar, Jyotsna Sekhar Shahane and Sita Khanna and my sister-in-law Indira Chaudhary Broome, all of whom kept me bolstered till the end.

And finally, to Janaki Visvanath, whose help I shall not forget, and Jaya Bhattacharji Rose, whose encouragement, editorial assistance and advice was the best any writer could have wished for.

ATIYA

Thirteen-year-old Atiya had been alone in the jungle all day. She had no wish to be with the other children in her class. School was awfully monotonous. The teacher droned in a one-pitch voice, and most of Atiya's classmates weren't listening. She couldn't even remember what the subjects were that day. Her classmates wouldn't miss her, Atiya was sure. They said she was slow and dim. They often made fun of her, and teased her. She was sick of them all.

Early that morning, she had dressed quickly, packed her bag with her usual tiffin, and yelled out to her father that she was leaving for school.

'Okay, bye!' Papa yelled back. He was too busy with his paperwork to come out and wish her a nice day. No one had much time for Atiya and that was the truth of it.

So when Atiya took the left path at the fork, nobody was around to see her walk in the opposite direction from the road that led to her school. She walked away, as fast as her awkward legs could take her, never looking back to see if anyone was watching. Her rucksack felt heavy on her back as she had packed enough to eat for the day. There were also two bottles of water, just in case she needed them. At a young age she had learnt to fend for herself. Limping along on her strong foot, the other being a little shorter, she used her wooden walking stick to balance herself. She was determined that no one, not even her dear Papa was going to stop her from getting away into the forest today! The path that she took was one that not many her age dared take. It led straight to the heart of the sanctuary. It was out of bounds as it was a dangerous place to be found alone in. It was home to elephants, tigers, panthers, hyenas, wild dogs, or *dhole* as they were calleds and even bear. That's not counting the venomous snakes that lived there too.

But Atiya was not afraid of the jungle. Her father, a Range Forest Officer, often took her in his jeep when he went out to make sure that his precious wild animals were safe from the poachers. She had grown up in jungle lodges in many South Indian sanctuaries. She was more comfortable with trees and wild animals around her, than with scores of loud, yelling, teasing children. The forest, for her, was a place of peace. A glorious green sanctuary, like it was for the wild animals that lived in it.

The sun had just risen when she reached the forest edge. A heavy chain hung across a mud road from one pole to the other. Locked! It was to protect the animals from being poached, or trees being felled and carted off in the dead of night in big trucks. Atiya knew that these things happened. Some sanctuaries, like the one Papa looked after were extra special. And Papa was a good man. No one could bribe or corrupt him. He was proud to have such a valuable and beautiful forest in his care. He had extra men to keep an eye on things. That helped too. Like their boss, this band of men was fiercely proud of their jungle, and though they came from all over India, they understood the responsibility of caring for 'their' jungle. They made sure everyone knew that they meant to do their jobs properly.

As Atiya walked along, she remembered Papa's instructions. 'It's the home of the wild animals,' he would tell her with a smile. 'We are only guests in the jungle. Like a good guest, you must be quiet and respect their space. No yelling, shouting, littering, chopping trees, stealing fruit or shooting any of the birds, animals or reptiles you may be lucky enough to see.' Atiya smiled to herself as she hobbled along, remembering that conversation. 'Yes, yes, Papa!' she had replied with a wave of her delicate fingers, 'I know what you mean.'

Ten minutes later, she turned a corner. She spotted a large clump of trees on the left side of the road. It was getting warmer. Tired from all the hobbling, Atiya decided to get a moment's rest. She leaned against a very and gnarled old teak tree. Phew! She was quite out of breath.

Faintly, she could still hear the sounds from the village about a kilometre away. The wind was blowing her way. The tinkle of cow bells, people's voices, a child wailing and even the horn of a passing vehicle. Her watch told her it was almost 9 a.m. It was the time when the rangers came into the sanctuary for their early morning patrol. She decided to get off the path and into the forest quickly or she might be spotted by a passing vehicle.

Her thirst quenched, and her bottle secure in her backpack, she hobbled on. Soon she walked off the main mud road, on to a side track and away from the village. She knew these roads like the back of her hand. This one was not too long—only two kilometres. After crossing another checkpost, it took you out of the sanctuary on the other side where across the river, there were a few tiled cottages. A popular jungle resort lay further down the road. She hardly ever saw either the owners or their endless stream of guests. The small homes and the resort were privately owned. Sadly, most of the cottages were empty, built by weekend visitors, who came to stay a couple of times a year. There were no walls, fences or barbed wire boundaries around them. Her father knew all the owners, but he was too busy to visit any of them in his free time. She often wished she could make friends with the owners, but like her father, Atiya had little free time for such things—what with school and homework.

The teenager was the only child of Forest Officer Ram Deva Sardare and his beautiful wife Sarojini. Atiya's parents had met in Dehradun and had fallen madly in love. Everyone warned Ram to think seriously before he decided to marry Sarojini. They said she was born to dance and would never be happy in a forest looking after just a home and family. Dancing was her life! But Ram was besotted with the beautiful lissome dancer. It was not long before he had swept her off her feet. They were soon married and set up home in a famous Sanctuary in South India. A year later, Atiya was born.

They adored their sweet baby daughter. Papa took her everywhere, teaching her all about nature. First it was the tiny ants searching for food and then it was the cute tadpoles in the puddles in every dip and hollow of the roads that they travelled together. He introduced her to army ants and fire ants, paper wasps and potter wasps, harvest spiders and giant *mygalomorphs*—the large hairy tarantula spiders that live in 'tunnels' in mud banks. He talked about snakes and their eating habits, their habitat and their prey. Sometimes as they walked together, he would hear a rustle in the leaves. They both knew it was probably a snake. On one occasion, he ran up to where the sound came from, squinted to get a good look and then pounced on a snake. Once it was a cobra, hissing furiously at him! Holding it by the tail, he showed Atiya its hood, spectacles and fangs. He told her that of all the snakes, its cousin, the King Cobra was probably the most intelligent. She knew that the Kings, as she called them, were rare, and she would cringe if she heard about someone having caught and killed one. Luckily, she knew several wildlife research scientists who were capturing them, multiplying them in captivity and then setting them free with their young in their own habitat again. She so hoped that the Kings would be saved from extinction.

Other than the tribal Kurumba children, there were few children in the forest. They often came by their lodge, as they walked through the forest, with their curly-haired unobtrusive parents. Barefoot and scantily clad, the tribals roamed the forests freely, hunting for berries and roots of indigenous plants and trees. As they had lived here for centuries, they had the right to some forest produce like honey and wild berries. Before she began to attend regular school, Atiya and the children sometimes played together.

Soon after her fifth birthday, while returning from a holiday in the hills of Uttarakhand, little Atiya contracted polio. Her parents were distraught. For almost a month, she lay in the hospital fighting for her life. The doctors in Mysore treated her in the nick of time—she survived. But they told her parents that Atiya's left leg would never be the same again. It had shrunk in size. In time, she would have to learn to walk with a stick. When she was stronger, she would require calipers to prevent her leg from collapsing under her.

At the time, Atiya never knew what anguish this had caused her mother.

When Sarojini married Ram, her dream to dance on stage was closed. But when Atiya was born, her ambition shifted to her baby girl. Soon, Saroj began to focus on teaching her daughter to be the best dancer in the world. While Atiya's father taught her everything he knew about the forest and its creatures, Saroj made her little girl learn all about rhythm, footsteps and movement. She introduced her to Carnatic classical music. The house resounded with the tinkle of ghungroos and tabla, sitar and singing voices. It was just a question of time and practice. Atiya would become the world's most sought after Bharatnatyam dancer—that was Saroj's dream.

But when Atiya contracted polio, it meant she could never be a dancer at all! Saroj's dreams were shattered. Heartbroken, within two years she left the family and returned to the city. The forest never had enough to keep her busy. The stage and dancing called her back like a magnet. When she left, she broke Ram's heart, but he knew there was nothing he could do about it. She didn't want to take her baby girl with her either. How could she? The stage and performances every week meant little time for home and family. Ram was thankful that his little Atiya, at least, was still with him. He dearly loved his little girl. He would not have been able to see her go away too.

Life slowly limped back to normal. But the house was suddenly silent. Atiya's father had had only one command after his wife left him—no music was ever to be played at home. He could not bear the pain and sorrow of having lost his wife to the dancing profession. He was determined that music must never influence his daughter or lure her to the stage too.

As the years went by, Atiya grew into a bright young girl. She had short, straight, black hair and a high forehead. However, she was far from good looking and her nose was way too long and pointed. Even her chin, was much too sharp in her bony face. She was a long, thin wisp of a girl—made for an athletic outdoor life, but was now trapped by her handicap. Even her ears, though small, stuck out at a ridiculous angle. People often wondered how such good-looking parents could have produced such an ugly child. But her eyes spoke of something else. They were exactly like her mother's— the most expressive eyes imaginable. And the longest lashes! In fact, they looked unreal.

At seven, her father took her off to the village school. The other kids were very boisterous. Their idea of fun was often to push and shove each other in the veranda outside their classroom. Atiya fell many times. She found it difficult without her walking stick. The kids would watch her floundering around trying to grasp the furniture in her attempts at retrieving it from behind or under a distant desk. She soon became the butt of all their jokes. Because her reactions were much slower than theirs, they called her slow and dumb.

But she was actually ahead of them in class. She had a natural bent for science and geography. Her father often had house guests who talked of expeditions they had been on all over India. They projected their slides onto a screen after everyone had dinner. On occasion, these sessions continued till past midnight. So it was natural that if her teacher at school asked a question on botany or zoology, Atiya's hand would go up first. Her grin and her friendly nature could move mountains. But she hadn't discovered this wonderful gift yet.

Now, as she walked deeper and deeper into the forest, she knew her classmates missed her not a jot. And not even her dear hard working father knew where she was. How she craved for a friend—just one friend. But other than Thampu, the eleven-year-old son of their Kurumba driver and that drivelling, snotty-nosed Suriamma, whose parents owned the only milking cow in the entire village, there really wasn't anyone at all. The others were either too young, or out working, or too old. Atiya sighed, deep in thought as she hobbled along the mud track.

Seconds later, she sensed danger, and her sixth sense took over at once. Something or someone was close by. Intuition told her it wasn't safe to be here. Quick as lightning, she looked around her. Nothing. Breaking the silence, a frightened peacock suddenly flew off, from behind a clump of bushes, miaowing furiously. What could it be? She was listening carefully. She dared not move. Running away was out of the question. Two steps and she would fall flat on her face. She had to think fast! Standing still, she hardly dared to breathe. Like a hawk, her eyes scanned the ground in front of her, to her right, to her left and then behind her. As she moved her head, her eye caught the movement of a blade of grass some ten feet away. It moved, ever so slightly. Some animal had moved this way, just minutes before her! She could see the outline of its footprint in the clump of grass. A bear?

Then she heard the animal. A very low snort, deep breathing and then a loud piercing squeal. It took all of her strength to keep herself upright, balancing her body with her walking stick. A sudden rapid movement and it was gone. It was a wild boar. She remembered her father's frightening experience on a jungle trip with his young rangers. 'We walked straight into a party of wild boars,' her father recounted that tale. 'They were feeding lazily in a clearing. Before any of us knew what was happening, a large aggressive male charged at us. Poor Madappan was right in front and could not get away in time. The boar lunged at him and using his tusks, it ripped out the man's' intestines in seconds. We just managed to get Maddu to the hospital in time. Wild boar can be verrrrry dangerous!' said her father. Atiya didn't move till the boar had been gone a good five minutes. She breathed a sigh of relief—a narrow escape!

Atiya decided to walk along the more open road again. In a few moments she was back on firmer ground. It was getting to be noon, the sun was already quite hot, and she looked for a cool shady spot to sit and have her lunch. She remembered a large boulder just a little further down, to the left of the road. It overlooked a dip in the forest, and was a good look-out point. She and her father had often sat on it.

The huge boulder had an odd shape—one side gently sloped up from the ground and it was easy for her to walk up it, to the top. The other side jutted out like the peak of the cap she wore. Below this peak, there was a cave and the ground at its mouth sloped down at least twenty feet. She remembered checking it out ages ago. Two enormous trees on either side gave the boulder oodles of shade and it was a perfect secret hiding place. Once she sat down on the 'peak' she couldn't be seen from any side at all. The entire area smelt of a large mammal. For all Atiya knew it could have been a bear, a panther, a tiger or a sambar—any one of these.

When she was comfortable, she opened her bag and ate her packed lunch at leisure. To a city dweller in the forest, the sounds of the jungle could be unnerving, especially if the source is unknown. However, for Atiya, these sounds were comforting. They were the music of the jungle and she loved every little chirp, whistle, bark, thump, twang, miaow and whirr that came with the breeze up to her seat on the boulder. It felt good to be here.

She happily breathed this wonderful clean air, enjoying the sensation of the extra oxygen in her lungs. The birds chirped incessantly. There were quite a few this morning. Woodpeckers *tocktocked* a tree right above her head as they did not seem to mind that she was so close. A serpent eagle flew overhead with a small snake in its claws, the snake still wriggling and trying to free itself. The bird was gone in seconds. A peacock and three peahens walked majestically at the base of the slope, thirty feet away, pecking at the ground. She had been told that they too ate snakes and were excellent to keep in large wild spaces where reptiles could be a problem to people. Every now and then, one would call out. What a raucous call, a loud MIAOW . . . MIAOW! This incongruous call was coming from a bird so beautiful that you could not help but admire its gorgeous blue green plumage. She was very proud of these fabulous Indian birds, and no matter how often she saw them, she would still marvel at the colours of their long, beautiful and graceful feathers.

Atiya sat there for at least an hour. From this point, the boundary of the sanctuary could not have been more than about 800 metres. She spotted a couple of small tiled roofs. Someone was scrubbing pans in the nearby stream. She heard people talking to each other.

The sun began to move down into the west. Now she knew it was time to head homeward. She had enjoyed the tranquillity of the jungle so much that she had not realized the time. It was slipping by so quickly. At her slow walking pace, it would take two hours to reach the village. The school would shut at 3:30 p.m. and she must be back in the vicinity of her home by that time or Papa would get suspicious.

She sighed—the jungle gave her so much inner strength that she did not want to leave. She picked up her belongings. With the aid of her walking stick, she climbed down the boulder carefully and walked back up the road. Thankfully, no patrol jeeps had come by. Very few animals could be seen along this stretch—it was too close to human habitation. If they came from this end, poachers had to trek for miles to get into the thick jungle. That is probably why the rangers did not bother to come this way too often.

Atiya got home just as the village kids charged out of their classrooms. Her father, still at the office, never saw her come in. The house was as silent as ever. The maid had swept and left hours ago. Dhola—her 'pedigree mongrel'—as she loved to call him, lay sound asleep on his back, oblivious of her arrival. Even he, lazy fellow, did not seem to care much whether she was there or not.

She was tired out and yet she felt revitalized. That night, Atiya made a decision—she had to do the trek again.

She heard a great horned owl hoot its spooky *Bubo! Bubo!* as it flew through the forest on silent wings. The stars sparkled at her, sharing her day's secret. Atiya was asleep in minutes.

A FISHING TRIP

Three months went by in a flash and the village school closed for the summer holidays. Atiya always looked forward to the holidays.

Today being a Sunday, Papa had promised to take her fishing. Angasammy, the cook, quickly made a packed lunch for the two of them and put three bottles of cold water from the fridge into a cool box. For good measure Atiya added a packet of chocolate and some banana chips. Outdoor trips always made her ravenous.

While he put two fishing rods into the back of the jeep, Papa got the gardener to dig up some worms which he would use as fish bait. Atiya threw in a bag with sun caps, a small rug and some lacto-calamine lotion——in case they were bitten by mosquitoes. Papa started up the engine, revving it up with gusto. Dhola sprang into the back of the jeep, barking with excitement. Atiya climbed carefully into the front, flinging her walking stick under the seat. As her father inched the jeep out of the front porch, still shouting orders to Manniar, the junior guard in charge for the day, Atiya saw the sun peeping out from behind the thick canopy of trees around their garden. The sky was clear with not a wisp of cloud. She looked forward to a super day with her father.

'Which way?' Papa hollered with an enquiring grin. The engine roared and Dhola's yappy barks added to the racket.

'The other side of the sanctuary, please . . . .*please*?' Atiya begged. She knew her father did not like to leave the vicinity of his beloved forest——but today was Sunday. He smiled at her indulgently.

'Okay, the other side!' Papa replied. 'But it's going to be a long ride, and we'll have to hunt for a good fishing spot. The riverbanks are sharp and jagged——it's not easy to get to the water there.'

'I'll just sit close by, even if I cannot reach it,' Atiya told him, happy that he'd agreed to her request. He was in a good mood. After a very long time, she finally had her father to herself!

The drive through the sanctuary was super. Their jeep bumped along on rugged and desolate mud roads. In the distance, a tranquil herd of spotted deer munched grass in an opening, undisturbed by the noise of the vehicle. Their white tails flicked up and down, registering their approach, keeping the flies away. The leader stood erect and still in their midst and watched them proudly. Only his tail moved every now and then.

A rat snake raced across the road in front of the vehicle and disappeared into the shrubbery. The deeper they went, the more peafowl they heard. Soon they were out of the sanctuary and on the other side. A family of Kurumbas ambled along—baskets on their heads. Papa knew them and waved cheerily. Thampu, the driver's son was with this group today and he yelled out at Atiya who looked back as they passed. She waved too. 'I'm going fishing!' she called out as they raced past them.

The road took them to the old iron bridge built in the late 1800s by British engineers stationed there at the time. The river, not so full at this time of year, was a lovely sight. Large boulders sat like cherries on a chocolate cake, decorating the sparkling waters that gushed around them. A tired cormorant dried its wings on a boulder after its swim—like a dhobi about to hang up his washing. Atiya saw a large fish jump out of the water and plop back in again. Moments later, they crossed the little group of tiled cottages. No one was about. The weekenders had not arrived yet.

The road wound its way along, hugging the edge of the riverside. They saw another herd of deer, drinking water at a shallow edge. A kingfisher bobbed his tail up and down as he sat on a low hanging branch on the opposite bank. She saw it dive in just as they drove by. He was lucky this time! With a squirming little fish clasped tight in its strong red beak, the bird flew off to a high perch to have his fishy meal.

'Fish for dinner!' Atiya whooped at her father. 'I know I'm going to catch at least one today.'

Papa laughed. His voice was, deep and loud. 'I wonder who is going to catch more—you or me?'

'The one that catches least, cooks dinner tonight.' Atiya yelled above the noise of the engine. Her father did not reply. He laughed again. They both knew Angasammy would cook it anyway. Papa did not know much about cooking, and was not too interested in food either. But, today was her day—he would keep a bright cheerful smile on his face. Atiya thought her father was lonely and was trying not to show it. She had no idea that Papa was worrying about something . . .

The fact was that lately, something was troubling him. With every passing day, Atiya was beginning to look more and more like his wife Saroj. Her eyes were exactly like her mother's. Though her smile was like his, Atiya had a mind of her own, much like Saroj— just as impetuous as she was too. Now at thirteen, Atiya was beginning to look like a young version of his wife. In a year or two, she would be very much a young lady—that was the part that was troubling him. Would she also decide that the city was where she wanted to be? If so, how would she manage with her handicap? If she decided she wanted to study in the big city, would she be able to stay with Saroj's sister Dips, in Bangalore? He did not think she could fend for herself, but once she finished her Board exams, Atiya might tell him she could. And then what could he do? He knew he would never stop her from following her own dreams, whatever they might be—even if it tore him apart. Still, he must not think about it. He must not let his worries show. Feeling guilty that he so often gave her so little attention, that he had decided today to give her a really good time.

The river took a turn to the left and he drove his jeep along the road that continued to follow its contours. He looked out for a gap in the bank, a sloping path to the river's edge, so that Atiya could get to it easily.

Eventually, he found the perfect spot. He slowed the jeep to a crawl, veered off the road and parked under a large tree, as close to the place as possible. Dhola leapt out in total abandonment, barking madly, followed more cautiously by Atiya.

'Oh, shut up!' she admonished the dog who would not stop prancing merrily around her. 'Come on!' he seemed to say. 'Get on, hurry!'

Atiya lay out the rug in the shade of a huge jamun tree. Together she and her father got their fishing gear in order. She never felt queasy hooking up the worms for fish bait. Fish had to eat too, hadn't they? Her father had brought her up like a boy—teaching her how to change tyres or learning about engines of jeeps or the insides of machinery was exactly the sort of stuff he wanted her to know about.

Pushing a couple of biscuits into a pocket, she walked carefully to a rocky outcrop and sat down. She swung her rod and line out over the water and saw the bait and hook plop neatly in the spot she had chosen. She waited for the fish to bite, allowing her mind to wander idly from one thought to the next.

Two more years of high school, and then she would finally be free of her teasing, thoughtless, classmates. She'd be fifteen then—Wow! All grown up! What should she study after that? Her father had suggested forest management in Bhopal, but she wasn't too sure about that. Something more exciting preferably, but what? Perhaps she could become an ornithologist, she was fond of birds! But studying them full time . . .?

She did like the idea of doing palaeontology—the study of ancient fossils, especially after her father, quite by chance, had discovered a huge fossilized tree trunk in the middle of a remote part of the sanctuary. It must have been millions of years old!

However what she was really interested in however, were the ways of the local tribal people. Perhaps that is what she should study—anthropology. But the nearest college of anthropology was in another state altogether. Her father would not be happy about that at all. She had decided not to discuss it with him until her final year was done. Who knew, perhaps another much more consuming interest might take up her fancy.

Papa had wandered quite a way down the riverbank by the time she stopped daydreamer. She could just see his head from where she sat, the end of the rod just visible and the line every now and then whizzing out, around his head and then back into the gushing, bubbling river, as Papa yanked the line out of the water to check for bait that had been nibbled clean, or hopefully, a fish that had been caught. No fish yet.

They spent a peaceful hour at the river side when all of a sudden there was a crackle of radio static from the jeep.

'Hello?' called a man's voice over the radio. Atiya recognized Manniar's hesitant voice. He sounded worried, 'Dorai, are you there?'

Atiya moved quickly. She pushed herself off the ground, with the help of her walking stick and was at the jeep in a trice.

'Hello?' asked Manniar again.

'Yes, Manniar, this is Atiya. Dorai is far away. Tell me . . .?'

The man sighed with relief. 'Atiya Madam, please tell Dorai to come back quick! There's been an accident . . . !'

Atiya sensed the man's agitation and sighed. 'What's happened? What accident?'

'Can't say. Please tell Dorai to come back soon! HURRY!' and the radio line went dead.

Atiya's hopes for a quiet day with her father came crashing about her. She hobbled to a point from where she could see him. Papa was deep in thought and looking very relaxed. She hated disturbing him, but she knew she had to.

'There's been an accident, Papa! Let's go back home!' Atiya yelled out to him. Unable to hear her, he turned but from her actions he knew it was something serious. In seconds, he had reeled the line in and come running up to where she stood. Quickly, she explained Manniar's call. They packed everything up and drove at a hell-for-leather pace back to the lodge.

Manniar stood on the porch, his eyes wild. Four Kurumbas stood patiently by his side, as if waiting for orders. They were Papa's regular tribal assistants in the Sanctuary. People of few words, they watched calmly as the jeep came to a halt next to them in the porch. One spoke, short and to the point.

'Accident, Dorai!' said one. He had wiry grey hair. 'The photographer . . . '

Papa slapped his own forehead with a resounding THWACK!

'Oh god!' he almost shouted. 'The German cameraman?'

All five of the men nodded mournfully. 'Dorai, you remember Rangappa, the tusker in musth?' He did not have to say another word.

Papa turned ash white. He clutched the bonnet of the jeep as he jumped out from the driver's seat in a flash. 'Where are the driver and the guide?' he asked them, calm and in control.

Work was calling Papa and Atiya knew he would soon be gone, not to be seen for the rest of the day. The men quickly crowded around him, all of them talking excitedly in Tamil. Atiya was quite forgotten. As they collected the fishing gear and the rest, and followed their master back into his office, Atiya was left to her own devices. In the hurry of her father's everyday work, Atiya as usual had little place. She sighed and followed them silently into the quiet house.

Sunday, for her at least, was over.

AN ACCIDENT IN THE JUNGLE

That night Papa told her about the accident.

A famous German photographer had arrived at the sanctuary guest house three days ago. His request—could he have a guide and a jeep for five days? He wanted some good shots of Rangappa, an old sanctuary elephant who had a bad reputation.

Rangappa was a loner. He had the longest tusks of any of the elephants in the area and a memory to match.

He disliked people and there was little anyone could do about that. The Kurumbas gave him a wide berth because he was usually grouchy and irritable. They refused to look for berries or go through the sanctuary if they knew that Rangappa was around. Everyone knew that the old elephant was unpredictable and not to be messed with. If they walked through the sanctuary after dark, the Kurumbas stuck to their regular routes. And if they ever came across a herd of elephants at night, along those routes, they would collectively yell, 'Ayyappa, po! Ayyappa, po!' Somehow the elephants understood the people's fear. Slowly and quietly the huge animals would walk back into the forest and leave the people alone. If, however, they came across Rangappa, the people forgot everything and just ran for their lives. Rangappa usually stood his ground with a terrifying rumble emanating from his throat. He seemed to enjoy the fear of the scurrying people. Rarely did he ever chase them, but he displayed a regular fondness for suddenly appearing, as if from nowhere and scaring them to death. As if to underline his potential ferocity, he would wrench a couple of young trees out of the ground, kicking up clouds of dust, make a mock charge, ears swinging wildly, trunk outstretched and trumpeting like a banshee. The entire proceeding would not last more than a few minutes, but once experienced, it was never forgotten!

The German wildlife photographer, Mr Kronhaage was well known. A couple of years earlier, Papa had seen an exhibition of his photographs. Kronhaage was an expert. He was meticulous, finicky, ambitious and very demanding—both on himself and the people who worked for him. However, it was certain that he was not the most popular of men.

'To cut a long story short,' said Papa to Atiya as they ate dinner, 'Kronhaage had spent three unsuccessful days following Rangappa in the forest. I told the guide and the ranger to be very cautious indeed. Every evening they would report about the demanding time that they had had in the sanctuary with Kronhaage. No matter what, he was never satisfied with his pictures.' Papa sighed, chewing thoughtfully.

' "One more!" Kronhaage would signal to the two men. "Just a few more!" and the whole day,' said Papa, 'the two men docilely followed Kronhaage, as he filmed Rangappa from a safe distance. This went on for three long tiring days. And still the man wasn't satisfied.'

Papa drank some water, and put down his glass. 'Then this morning, when we went off fishing, I warned our men to be sure to keep a safe distance from Rangappa, whom I now suspected was coming into musth. An elephant in musth can be a dangerous animal in the forest. Best left alone.'

Atiya knew this only too well and nodded.

'But Kronhaage had other plans,' continued Papa. 'He wanted a close-up shot of the animal, with the glands near its eye clearly "weeping" in his photographs. For a shot like that, the men knew he had to get way too close. They refused and warned Kronhaage many times.' Once again, Papa took a long gulp of water. Then he continued. 'Finally, Rangappa began to get more and more fidgety, as the sun rose in the sky and it got hotter and hotter. Kronhaage seemed oblivious of the animal's waving trunk and the low menacing rumbles from his throat. He continued taking his pictures. The men could not stop the photographer, as he picked up his tripod and moved in just one step too close. The next thing they knew—Rangappa had had enough. He charged. In five seconds, the photographer and his tripod had been lifted clear off the ground, whipped high into the air as if they were stuffed toys caught in the elephant's trunk and then—flung to the ground.'

Atiya gasped, only too aware of what that meant.

'THUD! STAMP! THUD!' said Papa, slapping the palm of his hand hard on the dining table. Their glasses and plates bounced, as if in agreement with the description. 'The guide and the driver turned and bolted. They didn't stop to look back. Anyway, Kronhaage wouldn't have lived another second.'

'Is Mr Kronhaage dead?' asked Atiya in horror.

Papa nodded emphatically. 'I drove the men back to the spot . . .' He stopped—his eyes looking distant.

'The place was in a total shamble!' said Papa after a moment's silence. 'Broken bits of metal, the casing of the camera and other equipment were strewn everywhere. A couple of trees had been uprooted and Kronhaage's body lay in a heap—unrecognizable, other than the torn green shirt and a dusty cowboy hat that lay untouched on one side.'

A heavy pall of gloom filled the room.

'Rangappa just got another victim.' said her father with fearful finality.

They ate the rest of their dinner in silence, each in their own thoughts. Papa had a lot of arrangements to see to the next morning. Telegrams, police reports to be filed, informing the German Embassy and Kronhaage's relatives and a statement to the Press.

Atiya could not help thinking of her lone trips to the forest. What if *she* came across Rangappa one day?

As she nodded off to sleep that night, she could hear a barking deer call in the valley—a warning call. Perhaps a tiger was stalking it. Had it managed to get away in time? The great horned owl flew by again—reassuring and capable, this nocturnal predator in the pitch dark of the jungle night. The crickets sang and the tree frogs croaked making a gentle conversation with each other. A night heron called from the stream close by. She heard a pair of village mongrels barking. As if in answer, Dhola barked back. Atiya drifted off to sleep.

A BANGALORE BREAK

In the first week of May, a long distance call came. The high pitched *tring-tring* echoed through the empty lodge that morning, waking Atiya with a jolt.

'Hello?' sang a familiar voice from the other end. It was her mother's youngest sister Deepti. Atiya whooped for joy. Deepti, who refused to be called anything but Dips, was a bundle of fun. She was Atiya's favourite aunt.

'Hello, Dips!' Atiya screeched excitedly into the phone. 'What's up?'

'Not much!' screeched Dips in reply. She sounded ready to burst into giggles any moment. 'But I wondered if you would like to come here for a bit of a holiday?'

'Wow! Wouldn't I?' Atiya hopped excitedly on her right leg. 'When?'

'Whenever, I guess.' came Dips', reply. 'Ask Papa to give me a call, when he comes home. We shall fix it up, okay?'

Atiya couldn't wait. This was exactly the break she needed. Once school began in a month's time, there was no question of a holiday. The routine of school everyday would return, and that was that—for another year.

Papa came home at lunch time. They chatted quietly. Atiya waited for him to finish his meal. When they moved to the drawing room, she brought up the subject of a holiday with Dips.

'Huh?' said Papa, a bit too gruffly. A frown had appeared as if from nowhere on his forehead. 'Why do you want to go to Dip's place? Is something special happening there?'

Atiya shook her head, but with a wide grin on her face—a grin that could move mountains. 'No, Papa. Dips thinks I need a holiday. Actually, so do I! Please . . . please?'

Papa could not think of a good reason why she should not go. He just knew that the house was like a morgue while she was away. But what could he do? He knew that his precious girl would have to leave some day, and he better get used to the idea. He grinned sheepishly. 'Alright. Just two weeks, that's all. I really cannot imagine. What I will do without you here. But go if you must!'

Atiya hugged him. 'I'll be back before you know it!' she told him and hopped off excitedly to her room as quickly as she could. She didn't want to turn back and see the resigned look on her father's face.

Dips called that evening to confirm Atiya's holiday plans.

'Tomorrow morning, Manniar will drive Atiya to Bangalore. She should be there by midday,' Papa told Dips. 'I'll arrange to have Atiya picked up in a fortnight—two weeks is long enough.' He grumbled at Dips, good-naturedly. Dips could be heard laughing wildly at the other end.

'Just two weeks?' Dips laughed. 'Really, Ram, you better learn to look after yourself a little more.'

Now it was Papa's turn to laugh. 'I learnt that a long time ago.' he said. To Atiya's tuned ear, it seemed more like sarcasm, but on Dips, anything—even open cynicism was totally lost. Dips lived in the present. Anyone who came in contact with her knew that there was no baggage, no hang ups, no regrets or resentments. Everything washed off her like water off a duck's back.

'Life,' she had once told Atiya, 'is full of "events". You can either spend your entire time with a woebegone face, resenting and regretting the sad and bad things that happen, or you can live through each "happening", thinking only of the positive and move on quickly to the next. Life is one big laugh. Get the most out of each glorious day and don't think back or beyond that day and time!'

Atiya knew that Dips, her crazy, funny and lovable aunt lived exactly that way. She had a fund of silly stories to tell at every turn. She could keep anyone amused with her idiotic jokes and anecdotes. Atiya adored the ground Dips walked on.

Manniar took her to Bangalore next day.

Dips was waiting at the front door of her spacious bungalow. She came running down the steps as the jeep drew to a halt, grabbed Atiya out of the vehicle and gave her a lung-squeezing hug!

'Oh boy! It's good to see you!' Dips said, laughing as usual. Atiya grinned. The laughter was infectious. She already knew that they would have a whale of a time together. The backpack and strolley were carried up the front steps in style and into Atiya's room. It was large, airy and light. It looked out on to a fabulous garden that never seemed to stop blooming. The plants echoed the non-stop laughter that floated out to them whenever Dips was around—it was a riot of colour! Mauves, pinks, pale pinks, yellows, oranges, and the orange pinks of the bougainvillea all along the edge of the garden, the floribunda roses in large buds and blooms of pinks and whites, and the day lilies in bright yellows and oranges. Closer to the large French windows, there were groups of clay pots placed at various heights, laden with pelargoniums in frilly reds and oranges, pinks and whites. In the shade right against the house, clumps of shade-loving variegated leafy plants waved their beautiful foliage in the gentle breeze. Even the plants seemed to smile at Atiya with their joy at seeing her again.

Over dinner, Dips and Uncle Dara discussed their plans for Atiya's stay.

'Dips, take her to the mela at Cubbon Park!' said Uncle Dara, chomping on his kaathi kabab with gusto. Dara was Sikh and a funnier man you'd never meet. He was the perfect partner for Dips. If it wasn't her, then it was he who kept their perennial guests constantly entertained. The Sikh jokes that Dara told were the latest, the funniest, but never the dumbest. And Atiya loved his wonderful ability to laugh at his own kind. Dara had often told her that if only Indians could see their own funny side, India would be the 'greatest nation in the world'!

Dips grabbed a piece of paper from her messy writing table and wrote 'Mela' at the top of a 'List of Must-do Things.' Pretty soon, the list had some twenty lines of Must-do's.

'But first, we go to Dr Gyan to find out about a new set of calipers for your legs,' said Dips to Atiya in a business-like way. 'That should not take too long hopefully. After that, we'll be all set to have a blast.'

For a fleeting moment Atiya wondered how they planned to have a blast with her leg in braces and going *thack-thack, clonk-clonk* on the ground as she tried to get walking with the new ones fitted on. Seeing Dips chewing hard on her pencil, deep in concentration, the thought was gone in seconds. She could actually laugh at the thought of the bangs, crashes and *thacks* as she imagined herself trying to walk steadily. Atiya visualized people being pushed out of the way, falling all over the place, as she dragged her metal braces through the crowds and traffic, faster and faster, better and better, till she floated like a model down a ramp, smooth as silk and fluid as a waterfall. She smiled to herself. She knew that it was wishful thinking, but it was fun imagining otherwise!

Dips made the appointment with Dr Gyan. They went to meet him the next day. He was very capable, asked all the right sort of questions, measured her height and weight and observed the way she walked. They had a very thorough session altogether.

Atiya walked on air as she left his clinic. Dr Gyan told her he would make her a pair of calipers that would be strong, reliable and would last her for at least five years. She'd probably need another pair by the time she became eighteen, when the bones in her body were stronger and more mature.

'Make sure you eat lots of food with calcium—have a glass of milk everyday,' Dr Gyan told her. 'You must maintain the strength of your legs. Exercise regularly, and if you can, get a physiotherapist to suggest a fitness regime that works for you.' He talked to her as if she was an adult. In many ways she felt like one.

The two weeks went by in a flash. Dips and Uncle Dara gave Atiya a super break. Two days before she was to leave, Dips took her to try on the new calipers. It was a perfect fit! The cold, hard metal felt uncomfortable against her thin leg. It grazed the lower part of her knee, but Atiya was so excited about it, nothing mattered now. At last, she had a stronger leg to stand on. She made up her mind to exercise daily. She must make the leg stronger. She had to try and get herself physically fit as quickly as possible, so that she could go further and further into the jungle as she had planned to do that first time.

Her holiday was soon over. Manniar came to pick her up in Papa's jeep. She hugged her aunt and uncle goodbye, climbed into the jeep, flung her walking stick into the back and off they went.

'It's a pity Saroj is away on tour in America, and could not meet Atiya now,' said Dips with a sigh, as the jeep vanished from view. 'I think she'd be proud of her tough daughter, wouldn't she?'

Dara nodded in agreement. 'Hmm, and she's going to be a very pretty young lady in a couple of years,' he said in total appreciation of his niece.

———

Papa welcomed Atiya back with open arms. He was happy to see her home. With school reopening within a week, they had to get the uniform and books ready. He noticed she had grown a few inches in the vacations. He was thrilled to see the way she was now walking with the help of her new calipers. She wanted to prove to him that she was growing up and could look after herself, no matter where she was. City or jungle, home or away!

THE NEW CLASSMATE

Atiya's classmates in her ninth standard were a little better than in previous years. She had decided that on the first day in her new class she would be nice to everyone, but would concentrate on her books.

'Why bother with the snide comments passed by your classmates?' Dips had told her with a twinkle in her eye. 'I bet, you'll find better characters in your study books.'

'You have two years more in school. After that, you stay with us and go to a college in Bangalore.' said Uncle Dara, eyes twinkling merrily.

'Yes!' added Dips. 'Medicine, dance, teaching, chess—anything you decide on. We'll get you started. Your Papa is glued to his job and the jungle, and he really cannot do much from there, poor man. But you know you can rely on Dara and me to help you. You only need to ask.' Atiya knew she would miss them, they were the best aunt and uncle anyone could wish for, but she also knew she couldn't do without her father; she loved him too much.

The new teacher was Mrs Naina Pillai. Her first lesson in geography was an eye-opener. Her students listened in rapt attention to every word she spoke; she had them eating out of her hand.

The last bell rang the school children out of their classrooms. Soon the playground was filled to the point of overflowing. Mrs Pillai watched her class pack quickly. They were out of the room in seconds. Only one student seemed to take her time—Atiya.

With calmness far beyond her years, Atiya packed her bag carefully, everything put away in its rightful place.

She slung her backpack onto a shoulder. Pushing herself up off her chair, she stood up. As she reached for her walking stick, Mrs Pillai realized why this child was last out of the class.

Quickly she walked up to Atiya and put her hand gently on her shoulder.

'I've been watching you all day,' she told Atiya with an apologetic smile. 'I didn't realize . . .'

Atiya shook her head and smiled back at the new teacher. 'I have new calipers, now,' she replied, in answer to the teacher's comment. 'I have to get used to them, but I can walk much better already.'

Mrs Pillai nodded, admiring this girl's tenacity. 'I like your spirit. You are an intelligent girl. If there's anything you'd like extra help with, you know you just have to come to me,' she said, 'anything at all!'

'Thank you, teacher,' Atiya said. They walked together to the door. Then Mrs Pillai left, saying she had a bus to catch. She lived in a tiny cottage on the other side of the sanctuary. As there was only one bus back in the evening, she couldn't afford to miss it.

Atiya realized at once that her new teacher lived in one of the tiled cottages just outside the sanctuary. She made a mental note of this important detail. She better be certain that Mrs Pillai never saw her walking down through that little hamlet, bunking school, or there would be trouble!

———

School turned out to be super that entire year. Atiya made friends with Mrs Pillai's son, Gopal, who happened to be in her own class. For a year, he would attend the village school for a special experience. Then he would return for his tenth class State Board examinations to Chennai. They discovered they both had a lot in common.

Gopal too was an only child. His father was the CEO of his own company and had little time either for him or his wife. He had divorced Naina years before.

'Dad's a very ambitious businessman,' Gopal had said, as Atiya and he sat eating their lunch during recess, soon after the school year began. 'He travels most of the time. He is always busy with his company,' he told her by way of explanation.

Gopal sympathized, when Atiya told him about her mother, who was by this time well known in art circles in south India. These two were already like young adults— well on their way to finding their feet and discovering their own talents.

'I think I'm going to take up botany,' he told her enthusiastically. 'The more I live near this sanctuary, the more I realize how much I love plants!'

Atiya smiled. She was familiar with plant lovers, wasn't she? Her father was passionate about only one thing in his life—botany. Atiya had inherited his love for plants. So she understood exactly what Gopal meant. 'Come and meet my father on Sunday,' she told him, 'He'll tell you so much about plants—information that you will never glean by reading a book.'

That weekend, Gopal took the bus from his mother's tiled cottage to Atiya's village. As it was a kilometre down the road, he walked from the village bus stop to her forest lodge. It was early. A couple of people walked in front of him, chatting quietly with each other. Gopal loved the peace that this forest seemed to give him. He absorbed it's calm as he walked along. Peafowl were everywhere. He heard jungle fowl as he came around one corner and saw a large rooster-like bird run back into the safety of thick cover as he approached. Two hens flapped away behind him and in seconds all three had vanished. Soon he was at the gate of the lodge.

A dog barked. 'Dhola, quiet!' ordered a familiar voice. Atiya stood at the front door, looking smart in her blue denim pants and a white T-shirt.

Gopal ran up the driveway. 'Hi!' he yelled as he came up to her. 'So, this is Dhola!' The dog wagged his tail furiously, approving of this new friend. Gopal heard footsteps and looking up, he saw Mr Sardare, towering over them.

Mr Sardare gave the boy a sharp, keen hawk's-eye stare. Gopal felt as if a steel rod had pierced him through and through and that his head had been peered into, every secret snatched out of him! Oddly enough he wasn't afraid of this man. He liked what he saw. Mr Sardare's grin—now he knew where Atiya had got hers from—made up for the hawks-eye. He had no idea that Mr Sardare had decided to stay home that Sunday just so that he could meet Atiya's new friend.

Gopal was average in height, but already he had the makings of a young man. He held himself well, his head squarely on his broad shoulders. His forehead was broad and his hair was dark, wavy and cropped really short— very practical. The boy had small eyes, thick glasses, broad capable hands and enormous feet—probably size 10 already—Sardare smiled to himself. Boys seemed to go through an awfully long, pimply, metamorphic phase. So unlike girls! His daughter, for instance, seemed to have turned into a swan overnight!

Papa and Gopal made friends instantly. The three of them walked back into the cool house, all of them talking simultaneously. Papa chuckled and clapped his hands, yelling 'Angasammy? Please get us some nimbu pani?'

They sat on the old fashioned but oh-so-comfy sofa and chatted happily. Papa's booming laugh echoed through the house, and suddenly everyone seemed to come alive. Gopal could see that Atiya's dad was everyone's idol, including his workers who looked up to him as if he was some sort of god. However Sardare himself seemed oblivious of this. He was quiet, capable, kind and a man very much in charge. He did not have much of a sense of humour, but then, neither did his own father. Gopal knew instinctively that he was going to like this man.

Papa, Gopal and Atiya talked for ages about the forest, the wild animals and the trees.

'How old are the oldest trees? Who planted them?' Gopal asked. Sardare gave him an amused look. This boy hadn't stopped asking questions since he'd entered the house.

'There must be some that are about a hundred, here, but the majority are about fifty years old,' said Papa in reply, 'Teak trees were considered very valuable, even then. Slow-growing, termite and insect resistant and hardy. The British realized their value years ago. They set up laws to protect our forests. Some of those laws exist even today!'

Angasammy came in with refreshments and mini dosas. He beamed at them, as they thanked him. Atiya let out a whoop! 'Dosas!' she screeched joyfully. Angasammy chortled in delight. He knew they were a perennial favourite with his Dorai and the little madam.

'Try them,' Atiya told Gopal. 'You'll love Angasammy's dosas. They melt in the mouth, I promise.'

The three of them ate heartily. Later, Papa took them for a drive through the sanctuary. Manniar and Dhola sat in the back. It was a gorgeous clear day and the first rains had tamped the forest mud down. The roads felt soft and smooth as they cushioned the tyres of the jeep.

A super smell of the forest after the first rains of the season filled their nostrils and they breathed deeply in wondrous silence. Atiya showed him hundreds of tiny red velvet mites, crawling all over the place. 'They emerge miraculously,' she told Gopal, 'immediately after the first rains.'

Gopal collected at least ten of them. He borrowed an old matchbox from Mr Sardare and stuffed them into it. 'I'm going to show them to Mum,' he told them in glee, 'She'll probably faint or something,' and he laughed.

A peacock flew across the road, in front of the jeep. 'Wow!' the three of them said together. They looked at each other and then laughed. This was turning out to be a companionable sort of day. That felt good. It meant that Gopal would be more often in their home and she would have a friend . . . finally!

PLANNING A TREK

Gopal often spent Sundays with Atiya in the forest lodge. Sometimes if he got information from a local informer, Papa had to go after a poacher. If it wasn't too dangerous, he would pile the two of them and Dhola into his patrol jeep and they would go racing into the sanctuary or around it, depending on where the culprits were hiding out or setting up animal traps, perhaps even stalking an animal.

Sometimes Atiya and Gopal would help ambush the thieves. If they were lucky, the poachers would walk unwittingly, straight into them and get nabbed by the forest guards. On one occasion, they chased a group of six men who had shot a tusker and sawn off its tusks. As luck would have it, a passing tribal chanced upon the group in the deep of the sanctuary. They were so engrossed in the heinous act of chopping up the animal, that they hadn't noticed him. The man ran back to Papa and told him what he had seen. Papa, the tribal and three guards jumped into the patrol jeep along with Gopal and Atiya and they raced through the inner forest roads, taking short cuts and catching the poachers in the nick of time. Had the poachers gone another hundred metres, they would have crossed the state border and escaped. The teenagers loved the excitement of the chase. If they were able to catch poachers, Gopal and Atiya would give each other a high five. 'One more bites the dust!' they would say.

By the time December came around, Gopal and Atiya had become good friends. They found it easy to tell each other their problems and often helped each other sort them out. They even had phrases and a handful of cooked up words of their own making, much like siblings within a family. None of their classmates understood what they were talking about much of the time. Homework became 'leech time', Hindi was 'mugger mucch' and 'ace-in-space' meant the highest score.

One Sunday, they sat under a strangler fig tree in the garden of the lodge. Papa had only recently told Gopal about the strange habit of this tree and the boy loved the story.

'The fig tree is a parasite,' Papa said, 'A seed may sprout close to any healthy tree, and for a while the rains will keep it growing. Then the fig tree begins to get greedy. It produces roots and shoots that gradually wind their way around the healthy tree, first under and eventually above ground.' Gopal looked at the thick entwining growth around the trunk of the jamun tree as Mr Sardare spoke. The parasitic tree was strangling it, slowly but surely, sucking the energy out of its host. 'The host tree will finally lose its strength and as the fig saps it of life, the jamun will gradually die, leaving a dead and hollow trunk.'

'Awesome!' Gopal gasped, 'No wonder they call it the Strangler Fig!'

'Yup!' Atiya agreed. 'In time, the hollow jamun trunk will become a shelter for smaller creatures and even birds . . .!'

'Such as . . .?' asked Gopal inquisitively.

'Squirrels, mice, rats, vipers and other snakes, and birds like barbets, woodpeckers, hornbills, owls . . .' Atiya rattled off with ease.

'Wow! An ecosystem!' said Gopal, envious of this knowledge of the jungle. Uncle Sardare called it India's 'valuable biodiversity'. Gopal longed to learn everything he could about this forest. The more time he spent with Atiya and her father, the more determined he became to finish school as quickly as he could and join the forest services. The jungle was the life for him!

Angasammy brought them tall, cool glasses of fresh *nira* juice, the sap of the wild date palm tree. Locals tapped it daily and sold it fresh in the early morning, as a cooling 'soft drink'. Atiya knew that if you stored it for a day or more, especially in the hot summer months, the juice would begin to ferment and pretty soon it would become 'toddy'—the local liquor that the tribals drank. It was cool and breezy under the strangler fig. A swarm of rock bees buzzed above in the canopy. A honey buzzard wheeled overhead and *kee-kree-d* his calls. Honey bees and hives were this large bird's daily bread. He would get a feast tonight, when the bees settled down to rest at dusk.

As they drank nira, Atiya turned to Gopal. She wanted to tell him about her trips into the forest.

'Do you like walking in the forest?' Atiya asked him as he sipped his juice.

Gopal looked up. Atiya had something important to say. 'Nope. Not on my own, anyway,' he replied with eyebrows raised, waiting for her to continue, 'I thought it wasn't allowed here. Why?'

'Just asked,' Atiya shrugged, smiling mischievously. 'What would you say if I told you I go often to the forest on my own?'

'Lucky you, I guess.' Gopal replied again, 'What's all this blathering about anyway, huh?'

Atiya checked to see if the coast was clear, then leaned forward in her chair. 'Can you keep a secret?' she asked.

Gopal grinned. 'Spell it out, man.' he said, keeping his voice down, but his grin gave the game away. This was beginning to get exciting!

Atiya described her jungle walks in enthralling detail. The paths she took, the animals she sometimes crossed, the encounters with occasional snakes, the nests of various birds and the tiny creatures on the leaves or the forest floor. Her descriptions were fascinating. Gopal didn't blink till she had finished.

He put down his glass carefully and looked at her. His grin got wider. 'So, when are we going?' he asked. His heart beat fast and he knew it would be disobeying rules, but this was one time he would not be telling anyone.

Atiya grinned, 'Well, your mother is my class teacher. We mustn't bunk school. So I guess it's got to be a Saturday or a Sunday.'

Gopal decided for the two of them. Saturdays would be safest. In any case, they were both halfway through the ninth standard; it was no time to bunk school.

'Okay!' Gopal said with another grin, 'We keep this top secret!'

'Done!' shouted Atiya in glee, 'Next weekend sounds good, what do you say?'

Gopal calculated quickly. He said. 'I'll catch the local bus to this village. I'll meet you at the end of your lane, at about 8:30 a.m., okay?'

'Done!' Atiya giggled excitedly.

They heard a state transport bus honking at the bus, stop down by the gate and Gopal jumped up. 'That's my last bus back. UGH! Okay, see you, Atiya.' He ran as fast as his legs could take him. The bus driver, a good-natured man, knew Gopal and Mrs Pillai well and revved his engine in playful fashion. He waited for Gopal to climb in and the bus set off with a lurch as soon as the boy found a seat.

Atiya waved from her perch on the garden seat. She was looking forward to their escapade next Saturday.

It felt good to have a friend at last!

CAVE ADVENTURE !

The following Saturday, dawn broke early. The sun peeked through the trees just a little. A fresh breeze blew. The air smelt clean and cool as Atiya and Gopal walked into the jungle.

Atiya had decided that the short mud track to the boundary through the left fork would be good for Gopal's first trek into the sanctuary. Later, they could become bolder, as he understood the jungle better—

learning to read tracks of animals, locate and identify bird and animal calls and be wary of venomous snakes, if he came across any of them.

They left the path and sat on the large peak-shaped boulder, just as she had done on many previous occasions. At this time of year the sanctuary was super, there was so much activity. The birds in particular, were everywhere.

They ate their packed snacks in silence. It was a quiet and comfortable comradeship that had grown between them over the past several months. A bird pecked and scrabbled on the grass down on the lower slope. Gopal got out the binoculars to check what it could be—long legged, stocky, hopping along on the ground from one patch to another, alone. Its colours fascinated him. The Indian Pitta. The first time he'd seen one close up was when, out in the garden on a weekend, he heard a sound like a gun shot. Seconds later he found a multi-coloured bird lying on the grass under the sitting room window. The bird had flown straight into the window pane, seeing the forest reflection in it and unable to judge reality from reflection, had slammed into it at breakneck speed. Gopal picked it up, but it was quite lifeless.

Next day, he showed it to Atiya who told him about the Pitta. 'The Indian Pitta migrates to south India in winter,' Atiya had told him. 'It's usually found on the ground, hopping about in big bounds, checking for ants and grubs on the floor, between leaves and vegetation. Very often, it's alone. And its call,' here, she puckered up her mouth and whistled the bird's two-note call— *pree preer,* the second note descending as she imitated its call.

Gopal listened in awe. 'Wow!' he said in admiration. One day, he decided that moment, he would be imitating bird calls just like she did.

They shared their snacks and drank water from their bottles. In spite of wearing caps, the sun was pretty much roasting their heads, when they heard a vehicle approach along the mud track. Atiya made a sign. 'Don't move!' she said and Gopal froze. Just when things were beginning to get interesting, someone had to come along and ruin the day. The patrol jeep, for that was what the vehicle was, carried on around the bend in the road in a cloud of dust. It stopped at the boundary, eight hundred metres further. Someone jumped out, unlocked the heavy iron chain across the road, the jeep drove through and the chain was yanked across and locked again. They heard men's voices and a mongrel barked from somewhere in the vicinity. Probably the occupants of one of the tiled cottages were at home and the dog must belong to them. Atiya knew only too well that a leopard's favourite food was a chubby village dog. You were unlikely to find a dog in these remote areas for they'd get picked up by a hungry leopard in no time at all! The sound of the jeep faded away and they breathed a sigh of relief.

'Papa's men often come to this same boulder,' Atiya said, 'to get an overview of the area. Good thing that they did not come here today.'

She got off the boulder and they dusted their denims. Both wore dull-coloured shirts as it camouflaged better in the jungle. That way you got to see more wildlife— hopefully before *they* spotted you!

'Do you want to explore a cave?' Atiya asked Gopal suddenly, as they clambered gingerly off the boulder.

'Of course!' said Gopal instantly.

Atiya led the way carefully down the slope, along the edge of the rocky outcrop, till they had gone almost a complete semi-circle around it. Now they stood at the lower ground level, directly under the peak of the boulder. Gopal gasped. A three-foot opening in the rock stared at them in the face. A cave! The end was dark and they couldn't see the inner wall, even when they shone a torch into it. They knew they had to explore further. This was too good an opportunity to miss. Atiya was her usual confident self. Her braced leg, now with the stronger shoe, allowed her a stable foothold on the ground and her limp was hardly discernable. However, she still held on to her walking stick. It gave her extra strength. Her physiotherapist had told her to keep using it, till she was sure she could do without it altogether.

Gopal took out his own torch. They flung their backpacks on the ground and crouched at the entrance, peering in, Gopal a little hesitant, Atiya daring him on. They sat on their heels, as she spoke softly, telling him about the cave.

'It's likely to be a mammal's den, but I can't say which—could be a leopard, a bear, a tiger . . .?' Atiya spoke calmly, but Gopal's heart was racing.

'In winter the animals usually come back to their cave or den around midday,' Atiya murmured quietly, 'They rest in their den until early evening, when it gets cooler. Then they'll come out and hunt for dinner.'

'How do you know one isn't here now?' asked Gopal, his eyes round as saucers. His palms were sweaty and shaking. He glanced at his watch. It was just after noon.

'I don't, actually,' said Atiya. 'But we can play safe by doing what some rangers do. We'll throw some stones in first. If there's no sign of an animal, after several stones, we can safely enter it. Okay?'

Gopal nodded. For a crazy moment, he thought about his Mom, who was oblivious of his whereabouts. He felt miserably guilty and yet so excited that the adrenaline was pounding like a demon racing through his veins. He knew he couldn't stop himself now.

While Atiya sat at the mouth of the cave, Gopal collected an armful of large and small stones. When he returned, Atiya pointed silently to the ground. It looked well used as the ground was smooth and flattened. The rock edges were smooth too. She spotted a clump of black fur stuck to a jagged edge of rock at the mouth of the cave. She looked at him—eyes wide.

'Some large animal definitely lived or lives here!' she told him excitedly. She took a small handful of stones from Gopal, and threw first one, then another into the mouth of the cave. They waited. Not a sound. Atiya threw another and then Gopal threw in one more. They could hear the stones rolling in quite a way, but no animal sounds. Atiya looked at Gopal and they decided it was safe to crawl in. 'We'll throw some more stones, once we get in further,' she told him quietly.

Their torches made sinister dark and light moving patches on the roof of the initial tunnel of the cave. They could just see their way in. Further inside, the ceiling receded. Once again, the back of the cave was dark. Gopal shone his torch from behind Atiya who had by now crawled ten feet further in. She threw another two stones. They could hear them rolling on, taking ages to stop. At one point the height of the roof rose steeply and they could stand here. It was dark, damp and smelt very strongly of some wild animal. They still couldn't see or hear anything.

'I guess there isn't anything here,' Atiya whispered to him. They threw some more stones further in. Now they spotted two separate tunnels, leading off this central high-domed section.

'Which way?' Gopal asked her. His heart pounded so hard, it felt as if it would blow itself out of his chest.

Suddenly, Atiya froze. For the first time she was a little unsure. She had heard a minute sound, but what was it? Could it have been her stone falling further? Or was it a low menacing sniff or snarl of an animal? They crouched in front of the tunnel to their right and shone their torches into it. Again the dark and light moving patches. All of a sudden, a loud, short, deep and terrifying growl filled the cave. A second later, a large dark furry creature came bounding out on four legs towards them and almost hit their outstretched torches. Probably momentarily blinded, the animal growled again. Then it bounded straight back into the dark depths of the den. Atiya and Gopal crouched like frozen statues, totally shell shocked. What was it? A bear? A panther? No time to think! They backed out of the cave as quick as they could, banging their heads on the low roofed section of tunnel. They groped madly in the dark, torches fallen by the wayside in their frantic fear and in a hurry to get out of the confined space as quickly as they could.

Outside, at the mouth of the cave, they grabbed their backpacks. Holding tightly on to each other, Gopal yanked her back up the slope the way they had come. It took forever, but they were finally on higher level ground. They bent almost double, hearts pounding in their chests, trying hard to get more oxygen into their lungs.

'Oh, boy!' said Gopal, his eyes still like saucers, 'That was deadly, man.'

Atiya, her shoulders shaking in silent, nervous laughter had had the fright of a lifetime. 'What was it, anyway?' she asked when she got her breath back. It was to remain a puzzle for the rest of their lives, especially since both knew they couldn't even ask an adult for fear of being caught disobeying sanctuary rules. They gulped their water, calming down slowly. At last, after an eternity, they began to make their way homewards.

As they approached the jeep track, a faint gentle sound floated across to them and they both stopped to listen. It was the sound of a flute.

'A flute? In the jungle?' Gopal said, looking bewildered. 'A little ghostly, don't you think?'

Atiya stood stock-still. The notes were almost ethereal in the calm mysterious atmosphere of the forest. Who could play the flute here, in the deep remote interior of the forest? For Atiya, the sounds were almost supernatural. Ever since her mother had left her and returned to the city, she hadn't been allowed to listen to music at home; any music—classical or otherwise. Papa had insisted on it.

Now, after so many years, here she was, listening to a glorious melody. Someone deep in the forest was playing the flute. She imagined an angel playing the wood-wind instrument using the canopy of the trees like a natural surround sound system. The notes floated around her and engulfed her utterly and completely. It was pure, blissful and sweet!

When it was over, she was unable to speak for a while. Gopal looked at her, a little out of his depth at her unusual behaviour. Gone was the boisterous impetuosity of his friend. She looked solemn, very serious indeed.

'Wasn't that lovely?' Atiya asked him when the last notes died away.

Gopal shrugged, 'It's music, after all!' he replied, 'Come on, we better get home!'

Atiya shook herself alert again, as they walked back down the road. She did not know it now, but that flute was soon to change her life.

DISAPPOINTMENTS

The jungle visits had to stop after the cave adventure. The final exams were around the corner. Both Atiya and Gopal knew they must study.

But each night, after study and work were done, Atiya remembered the sound of the flute. It became an obsession. She knew, like everyone else in her father's house, that music was taboo at home. Papa would hate her for even suggesting that she would like to learn to play an instrument, let alone the flute!

But the sound of that flute, it wouldn't go away. Finally one day mid-April, after her final exams were over and the summer vacations had come around again, she broached the subject.

Angasammy served them their favourite mini dosas at breakfast. Papa's day had not yet begun. They chomped away merrily. Atiya's last morsel swallowed, she picked up enough courage to speak. Papa looked at her. Atiya had a tiny frown between her brows. The grin was gone.

'Papa?' said Atiya, clearing her throat.

Sardare could read her thoughts. Had the dreaded moment finally arrived? Was he going to lose his precious daughter now? Would she say she wanted to go to town to study?

'Papa, I . . .I heard some music the other day. I wondered . . .'

Sardare interrupted, his face like thunder. 'What music?' he almost shouted. Angasammy nearly dropped his plates and Dhola scurried from the room. Everyone knew that the master's anger was frightening. Atiya, however, held her ground. She had just one thought in her head. The sound of that flute!

'I heard the flute some days ago. It was . . .', she searched for the right words to describe her feelings, 'awesome!'

Papa looked at her distractedly. He hadn't expected her to come up with anything like this. 'Flute?' he snorted at her, 'Awesome! Where?'

Atiya waved her fingers in the air vaguely. 'Can't remember, but . . . Papa, may I learn to play the flute? Please?'

'But who will teach you, Atiya?' he asked her, 'I don't know of anyone who can teach you *here*!'

'Dips could find someone in Bangalore, I'm sure!' Atiya said in a rush, 'I could learn during the holidays?'

Papa shook his head and banged the table with his fist. 'NO!' he shouted at her. 'What will you do with the stupid flute? How do you expect to earn a living with it? It'll fetch you nothing!'

Atiya pleaded again, 'I could learn to play in Bangalore, then come home and finish my tenth class examinations here. I know I can practise on my own, once I learn the basics?' She tried grinning, hoping to melt his iron will, but Papa didn't budge.

'No!' he said again, 'And that's final. I refuse to see any more of my family ending up on stage. Not after your mother vanished with her dancing ambitions. No way!'

'But Papa,' Atiya said calmly. 'I'm not interested in going on stage. I just want to enjoy *playing* it, that's all.' She spoke from the heart, but Papa didn't want to hear another word. He shook his head, got up quickly, threw his napkin down and stamped out of the room. Atiya choked back her frustration and her tears. Why didn't Papa try and understand her longing to play the flute?

—

Atiya sat in the garden, under the strangler fig in her usual chair, after breakfast. Her thoughts were distant, as the village bus screeched to a halt down by the gate. She didn't hear two voices, until they came closer. Looking up, she saw Gopal and Mrs Pillai walking up the garden path towards her. She got up to greet them, forgetting the flute for the moment. It was good to see Gopal again. 'Good morning, Mrs Pillai!' Atiya grinned at the two of them. Gopal looked a little glum.

'Hi, Atiya!' they said together.

'We've come to say goodbye,' said Gopal for the two of them.

Atiya stood still. 'What?' she asked. Then she remembered that Gopal had told her he would be here only for one year. Two disappointments in one day was just not fair!

Mrs Pillai stood on one side, letting them finish this exchange first.

'We're leaving for Chennai,' explained Gopal. 'My one year here is up. I have to finish my tenth class in Chennai. Ma says I need tuitions for physics and chemistry. I will not be returning for the final year here.'

He told her he would be staying with his father, 'If I get time, I'll come and visit Uncle and you during the winter vacation.' He explained, 'Ma will come back here. She says she cannot abandon all of you at this crucial time.' Gopal grinned at her. Atiya breathed a sigh of relief.

Thank goodness for that.

They joked about the crazy fun they had had that whole year and even hinted broadly at some of their jungle escapades. Mrs Pillai was only half aware of this conversation, and the chuckles and secrets between these two. She was watching the tall man driving up in his jeep. Mr Sardare had just returned home. Seeing them in the garden, he jumped out of the jeep and walked across the grass to them in long quick strides. He shook hands with

Mrs Pillai and introduced himself. The children watched as Naina smiled at him.

'Is it actually you, Ram Sardare?' Naina asked incredulously, 'Weren't we in college together in Coimbatore?'

Ram took a step forward, in surprise, 'Yes, that's so. I studied botany there and then shifted to Bhopal for the last two years. Were you in Coimbatore College too?'

Gopal's mother smiled again, 'Yes, I was there for three years, but then I moved away to Chennai.' She shook his hand, 'I'm Naina Narayan.'

Sardare looked at her, squinting a bit, 'Were you in that crazy play with the eccentric psychiatrist and the four students . . .? Were you one of those students?'

Her nod and smile told Sardare that he was correct. He grinned in delight. 'I had a crush on you, never did get to tell you that, did I?'

Mrs Pillai laughed. She looked young and fresh in her pale blue sari. It wasn't difficult to see why Sardare had had a crush on her so many years before.

'How time flies, hah!' Sardare said, 'What finds you here?' When she explained, Sardare exclaimed, 'I never knew that Atiya's favourite teacher was the Naina of my college days!'

Everyone laughed and they sat down to enjoy freshly brewed coffee together. No South Indian home was complete without the smell of fresh ground coffee floating out of the kitchen. While their parents chatted, catching up on old times, Atiya and Gopal made quick plans.

'Write to me.' Atiya demanded of Gopal. 'I'm going to miss you here.'

'Yup, me too. I will write, I promise.' Gopal replied, giving her a high five, 'No treks without me, okay?' His solemn expression made her realize that he was serious.

'Well, right!' Atiya chortled. Sardare, who had overheard the word 'treks' looked from his daughter to Gopal. The boy, he noted, was grinning mischievously. Sardare made a mental note to ask her more about this later, when they were alone.

They could hear the State Transport bus approaching, the wheeze when the driver pressed the air brakes. Then it came round the two hairpin bends, at the base of the small hill, below the forest lodge, the noise echoing up to them each time. The bus would soon be at the village stop. Atiya's heart was heavy as she said goodbye. Who knew when she would meet her dear friend again? It might be years. And there was still so much they could have shared. Well, it would simply have to wait till they started writing to each other. Other news about him would probably come through Mrs Pillai once she returned at the beginning of her final year. Better than no news of Gopal at all.

'I'll be back,' Gopal said, grinning cheerily, 'You'll see!'

She sighed, waving a thin delicate hand at the two of them. The bus suddenly came round the corner and screeched to a halt when the driver spotted the Pillais. Angasammy helped them put their luggage into the bus.

'Bye! Take care!' they were all saying together, and with another screech of brakes and engine, the Pillai's were off.

Atiya sighed again and turned away. Without Gopal for company, this vacation was going to be a ghastly bore.

She wished Dips would call. But Dips and Uncle Dara were planning on a foreign trip this summer. That meant no Bangalore trip, for some time to come. Atiya saw her dreams of playing the flute fly out of the window. She walked back to the house with a heavy heart.

THE OGRE AND THE SAINT

The vacations began with sweltering heat.

The main road through the sanctuary became an endless stream of vehicles driving on towards Kerala, all packed with vacationers. They descended in huge numbers in cars and buses, honking madly at every corner and scaring the wildlife off the roads and forest edges altogether. For seasoned foresters, this time of year was rotten. In spite of huge posters proclaiming the sanctuary to be the home of the tiger and the elephant, and please not to litter, Atiya's father and the other rangers grumbled non-stop about the filthy habits of their fellowmen.

'Disgusting and thoughtless!' one ranger would say. 'And selfish!' another would add.

Papa would moan in frustration, 'Why cannot we Indians learn to be more civilized?' He would wave his fists at a bunch of visitors, as they flung out beer bottles and plastic bags of litter. 'Do they ever think about our dwindling wildlife?' he would say, whenever the rangers returned from within the sanctuary, after the last patrol of the day. Always with a sackful of litter left behind by passing travellers—cold drink bottles, beer, papers, chocolate wrappers and whatever else the passing motorists didn't want to be stuck with! Sometimes, a strong gust of wind would sweep up plastic bags with the remnants of snacks stuck in the corners and the next moment the same plastic bags ended up jammed in tree branches. They were an irresistible temptation for a passing herds of elephants, deer or bison. All animals need some salt in their diet, so plastic bags with salty leftovers become a potential threat—or treat—depending on which way you look at it.

'My poor elephants don't know how to get the salty crumbs *out* of the bags, so they finally end up swallowing the bags!' he would tell his men, as they would spend hours clearing the jungle of plastic bags. This was not their job, but they loved and valued their wild animals enough to get down on their hands and knees and collect someone else's garbage. 'Pathetic!' Papa would groan.

One Sunday after their last guests had left, Atiya decided this was an opportune moment to plead with her father once more about flute lessons. 'Papa,' she began. 'You remember I asked you about flute lessons?'

Papa nodded, taken aback that his daughter could change the subject so quickly. 'Yes, I do. What of it?'

'Well, I wondered if you would let me learn during my holidays?' Atiya asked softly, fearing a torrent of angry scolding from her father.

Papa, strangely, was very quiet, as if in deep thought. When he spoke, it was as if he was talking aloud to himself. 'Just like her mother!' Papa muttered, 'Once she has a bee in her bonnet, nothing can stop her. She'll have to go to the city if she wants to learn music. What will I do if she goes away too?'

Atiya jumped up and gave him a consoling hug. 'No, Papa,' she told him, 'I don't want to go to the city. Can't we find someone to teach me here—just during the holidays?'

Papa sighed sadly. 'Are you also going your mother's way? Music, dance, the stage? I cannot stand the idea of losing you too!'

'I'm not interested in the stage, Papa!' Atiya said, her grin taking him by surprise. How come he hadn't noticed her grin before. 'I just want to play the flute!' Papa heard her say.

Sardare unable to resist her pleas any further, finally agreed to try and locate a teacher for her as soon as he had some time. 'But in a few days, Atiya, I have urgent work on the other end of the sanctuary. I'll be away the whole day. Tell Angasammy not to make me any lunch. There are poachers about . . .' And he pushed back his chair, jumped up and with a tender pat on her head, he began reading the Sunday newspapers.

Atiya missed Gopal more and more each day. What were the holidays for, she wondered, if not to have fun with friends, enjoying their company and doing things together?

❦

Next morning after Papa left, she decided to take another walk in the forest. Papa wouldn't return till late in the evening. Quickly, she packed up the leftover breakfast, put a generous blob of tomato ketchup on the top, shut the box, filled two bottles of water and, with her cap and her stick, she left the house.

She had soon crossed the chain link checkpost that led into the heart of the sanctuary, walking along at a steady pace. The calipers were a boon. Her legs had gradually improved in strength with the physiotherapist's exercises that she had been doing daily for nearly a year. She would always have a slight limp, but her back was straighter now and though she still needed the stick occasionally, her dependence on it, without her realizing it, had become less.

Her face was not as thin as it had been earlier. Now, at fourteen, she was beginning to fill out, and her nose, at first glance much too long and pointed, was beginning to 'fit' the proportions of her face. Even her chin wasn't as sharp as it had been just a few months ago. Dips had suggested she grow her hair, which Atiya had done. It now hung down straight to her shoulders, not a bit of curl in it and jet black. In the sunlight, it shone like black glass! Even Gopal had commented on it once, just before he went back to Chennai. She sighed. She missed her friend!

As she walked along, she noticed her strides had increased. Idly she wondered if she had grown taller too. When she reached the boulder with the peak, she flung her backpack down, and grabbed an overhanging branch to swing impetuously on it for a moment. She couldn't do that last year, she must have grown four inches. Wow! The joy of being here in the forest, even if she was entirely on her own, was something not to be missed.

Stopping only a few minutes to finish the leftovers and drink some water, she continued along the muddy track taking the left fork at the usual place. Thirty minutes further, she had reached the chain link fence at the other end of the sanctuary. Once again, the tiled roofs of the little cottages came into view on the riverbank opposite. Surprisingly, no one seemed to occupy any of the homes, she couldn't hear a sound, not even a dog barking in the distance, or the sound of human voices.

She clambered over the chain and walked out on to the tarred road on this end. In the distance, she spotted a freshly painted signboard, on the edge of another track. 'Big Bear Lodge—5 km', it said in bold letters. 'Visitors welcome!' That was the holiday resort that she'd heard so much about. There were constant visitors there all year round. It was noisy and some of them came armed with radios and MP3 players. Noise, noise and yet more noise. Her father often said that Indians could not do without some form of sound all the time. Of course, that was just his way of telling her, that the silence in the jungle is really the opposite. It's to be taken advantage of——it rejuvenates, gives one peace and a sense of quiet contentment. Ah, well, not everyone was like her father, she knew and smiled to herself.

She decided to continue along the main road. A couple of vehicles hummed along some distant ghat road, the drivers revving their engines as they approached hairpin bends or difficult stretches. Oof! She would hate driving a vehicle like a heavy truck up and down those infamous roads. Thank goodness she was lucky enough to live in the heart of this gorgeous sanctuary, surrounded by peace and quiet and with time enough to continue her own hobbies. In just twelve months time, this phase of her life would be gone forever. She wondered what the years ahead would bring. Would she have moved to the city, after all? Would she be living in a hostel, or perhaps with Dips and Uncle Dara? She was still utterly confused about what she wanted to study in college. And Papa was no help with these things. He probably would have liked to have them frozen in time forever, never growing, never changing, never moving on . . .

She walked along, in the shade of the trees on the edge of the road. Suddenly a sambar stag jumped down from a rise. He spotted her and bolted. In seconds he had vanished. A peacock called and answered. Then she heard the gurgle and rush of bubbling water——the river. She walked a little faster. The water was a source of endless wonder to her as it swooshed between the larger boulders in the river bed calling to her as she approached the bank. 'Atiyaaaa! Ashshshshshiyaaaa!' it sang its cheery cool melody.

On the other bank, she spotted a tiled cottage in the distance. As she sat to take in the marvellous view of the sparkling gurgling water, she heard another sound. Human voices! She couldn't spot anyone, so where were the voices coming from? Very gradually, one voice rose in pitch and decibel level. It was a man's voice, rising higher and higher, more and more terrifying as the seconds turned into minutes. She could hear another voice now, a female and pacifying voice, calm and caring. It was as if the pacifier was attempting to calm the man. Atiya squinted, shielding her eyes from the sunlight. Still no one in sight. Where were the voices coming from?

She raised a wet finger to the wind and felt it as it cooled and dried. The wind was blowing from across the river, where the last tiled cottage stood, a little distant from the rest. It was almost hidden by the trees around it. The voices too must be from there.

As she got up to take a better peek at the tiny green space at the back of the house, an old man came hesitantly out of the back door. He was yelling angrily at someone indoors. Every now and then he looked back towards the house, waving his arms about, grumbling, mumbling. He looked irritable and upset.

Atiya stood still. She felt as if she was trespassing on their space and yet she couldn't move away. The man wore dark glasses and had a walking stick. He was bent almost double and walked hesitantly. He moved barely five steps and stopped, rooted to the spot. What was wrong with him?

Suddenly the calm voice called. Seconds later a thin young woman came out after the old man. She held a chair in her arms and walking past the old man, she placed it firmly on the green grass, under a large arjuna tree. Then she went back to the man, held him by the arm and led him to the armchair.

'Oh, Father! Tch, tch, tch,' she said quietly, took away his stick and gently pressed him down into the chair. She gave him a kiss on his cheek, smoothed the few strands of hair that remained on his bald head and walked back into the cottage.

The exchange didn't stop there, however. Atiya watched fascinated as the old man grumbled, snorted, riled and fumed at the invisible figure indoors. He yelled at her, demanding first some water, then a glass of juice, his book and something else. Each time the young woman would emerge, give the old man what he wanted and disappear inside again. And each time she spoke to him, it was with tenderness and love. Was she oblivious of his raving and ranting? How could she patiently answer his angry comments with calm and peace in her voice and manner?

What an awful bully the old man is, thought Atiya to herself. She grimaced. Who would want to look after a grumpy old dodderer like him? Atiya was sure the young woman was a saint. What were these two doing at the edge of the sanctuary? Not locals, that was obvious. They spoke a different dialect, and she couldn't quite identify it. Where were they from? She wondered how she would ask Papa more about them, without him discovering her secret trips to the jungle . . .

Suddenly, she remembered the time and looked at her watch. It was past three in the afternoon. She realized with horror that it would take at least three hours to get back home. Papa would definitely be there before her arrival. She walked back quickly to the tarred road, where the other empty cottages stood. In a straggly line and caught the last bus back to her village. The driver was mighty surprised to see her get into his bus as he didn't remember bringing her on his morning trip—perhaps her father had dropped her here on one of his patrols?

'Good evening, little madam!' he greeted her as she gave him a rupee for her ticket, 'Saw any wildlife?'

Atiya gave her usual cheery grin, and shook her head. 'No!' she told him, monosyllabic. She wished he would leave her alone.

'That's odd,' replied the driver, 'I almost slammed into Rangappa the rogue elephant, on my way down this morning. We had to stop for forty-five minutes, on one corner, till the old guy gave up his game, turned around and went back into the forest. Don't know how you missed him,' said the driver, scratching his head in disbelief.

Atiya grinned and let it pass. Better get home as quick as she could. Rangappa and other such problems later.

She walked into the quiet house fifteen minutes before Papa returned. He was too tired and dusty to ask her any questions. Both pretty exhausted, they had their dinner and retired to their own rooms.

As she clambered into her cozy bed, the fan above whirred and creaked like an old cranky machine. She kept hearing the old man's grumpy voice and wondered how anyone could tolerate such an awful person. What sort of evil guy was he? And, how was she to find out more about him?

As luck would have it, Sardare had to attend an important meeting in Mysore with the Chief Conservator of Forests the very next day.

'I'll be away overnight,' he told Atiya. Mysore didn't interest her in the least. She had other plans.

'Don't worry about me, Papa,' she told him, 'I'll be busy. There are a couple of other things I have to do.' She gave him a hug and her usual grin. Papa relaxed.

He left next morning, promising to return as soon as the meetings were done. 'Don't you do anything stupid or dangerous, Atiya!' he warned her as he hugged her goodbye, 'I'll call you this evening. Look after yourself.' As he leapt into his jeep, and disappeared down the drive and out of the gate, he had no inkling that his headstrong daughter already had a plan in place.

Atiya couldn't wait to find out more about the Ogre and the young woman she had seen on her previous visit. There was something strange about them. She must check them out and return on the last bus, as she had done the previous day. No one would know where she went, except the driver.

Angasammy packed a solid meal for her and with the two bottles of water, her backpack was heavy. 'Thanks, Angu!' Atiya smiled at him, 'I'm going to the village library, as I have some reading to do. I'll be away all day and will return at about six in the evening,' she told him, as she walked down the porch steps, one at a time.

Trusting old Angasammy! The man nodded his wise head at her and said quietly. 'You stay safe.'

No one saw her walk down the left fork. Dhola followed a short distance, but when he heard a strange sound he scampered back home as fast as his legs could take him. The birds were out in large numbers this morning. The courting and mating season had begun and there was furious activity everywhere. She saw the racket-tailed drongo swooping between the branches with its mate; they looked lovely flying together like a pair of acrobats in the air. Hill mynahs screeched a raucous warning as she walked past. Jungle spies! If you heard them screech, you could be sure they had spotted a wild animal or a human. Looking up, she saw at least four of them on the top of an old teak tree. Several holes in the bark gave the game away. They must have laid their eggs, perhaps the nestlings had already hatched.

Further along the mud track, she saw a small herd of spotted deer, grazing peacefully. There were many females and three very young fawn. Not far away, looking very much in charge, stood their proud father. The tips of his fresh antlers shone like a golden crown, lit by the eastern sun behind him. Atiya admired him and smiled. He watched her approach and then with a snort, he moved three steps. Next moment he and his family bounded away on thin delicate legs, sailing over the bushes, light as a feather! One minute they were there, the next. They had vanished.

Atiya breathed in the fresh clean air. Last night's rain had swept away the dust, and her shoes scrunched on the tiny pebbles as she walked. The teak tree leaves, huge and weary looking the last time she was here now looked perked up and fresh again. The smell of wet soil egged her on, filling her nostrils like heady wine. She loved the smell of wet mud.

Little green tufts of grass sprouted everywhere. As she walked further into the forest, she saw the huge clusters of common gulls, the bright yellow butterflies that gathered in huge numbers at this time of year. They dotted the muddy buttresses of the trees. 'Mudpuddling,' Papa used to call this activity. Hundreds and hundreds of butterflies—fluttering about, spreading and closing their pretty wings, reminding Atiya of miniature gardens of yellow flowers, their petals moving gently in the early morning breeze.

Atiya reached the riverbank in a couple of hours. She sat down, tired and hot, on a granite rock. Opposite her, she could see the last tiled cottage. Its tiny patch of green grass in the back garden looked so inviting. She took out her packed lunch and leaned against the trunk of an old tree. The aroma of her lunch made her mouth water. Thank goodness for Angasammy, she thought to herself.

'Vacations and treks,' she thought to herself. 'Hmm!' she sighed contentedly. A couple of jungle crows alighted on a branch above her head, cawing noisily. She couldn't shoo them away, and finally gave up, ignoring their racket.

Suddenly, she heard a shout. The Ogre! He had begun his ugly, bad-tempered harangue again.

'I don't want to eat this stuff!' she heard him say. His voice echoed over the riverbank and straight across to where she sat. 'Why do you keep giving me this slime?'

'Papa, it's for, your own good, you must eat it,' Said a female voice, in a cajoling reply. 'You know what the doctor said. And it isn't slime! Now please finish it off!' Their conversation was half in English, and half in a local dialect. This time she was able to get a gist of their speech.

'You're after my blood, I tell you!' grumbled the Ogre loudly again, 'I don't want it. Take it away!'

'Oh, please, Papa!' came the low, calm voice. This young woman really was a saint 'For my sake, then?'

'Your sake, my foot!' ranted the Ogre. 'I don't want to live any more. You are a bully! Demanding, horrible and useless to me! I don't need you any more.'

Atiya would have loved to give the old man a mighty swat with something. Shut him up for a bit! That would teach him a lesson! Why was he so awfully grumpy, she wondered? And why was the Saint so kind and good to him? This old man needed someone to teach him a lesson or two. The more Atiya heard, the angrier she became. How dare he be so rude to that poor woman. Who did he think he was, anyway.

Atiya had no idea that the two of them were soon to play a very important part in her life.

A SURPRISE

Atiya sat on her rocky perch and watched. A few minutes later, the young woman came out of the back door, carrying the armchair. She placed it, as usual, in the shade of the tree, making sure its four legs were steady on the uneven ground. Then she went back and brought out the Ogre, holding him gently by the arm as she led him slowly to the chair. The Ogre held a walking stick in his right hand. He had his dark glasses on his beaky nose. He used the walking stick. Suddenly it hit Atiya—

he must be blind! For a moment, Atiya felt a twinge of remorse. She watched the woman go back inside. Poor old man, she thought. The young woman had mentioned medicines and a doctor. Perhaps he was unwell. But the pity Atiya felt for him vanished in minutes, for the Ogre was ranting again.

'These stupid ants!' he shouted. 'Why do you always place my chair on the ants' nest? Stupid woman!' Atiya watched as the Ogre bent to scratch at his ankles. He hit wildly at the tiny creatures biting him, flailing his arms around, shouting out rudely, 'Get me away from here!'

The woman came rushing out of the back door, looking harassed. Her hair untidy and her apron still untied, she ran to the old man, pulling him up and out of his chair again. She picked up the chair, moved it to another spot, and once again, led him gently to it. 'Papa, oh Papa, dear, I am so sorry!' she said in her gentle voice.

Atiya watched the scene, growing more frustrated every minute. She wished she could fly across the river to the other bank and whack the ogre as hard as she could. How rude and thoughtless could he be—and when would this dear woman give up, and ignore his ranting and raving for a bit? How Atiya hated the old man!

The noisy scene on the other bank did not stop for the one hour that she watched the pair of them. Finally, in disgust, she picked herself up. She'd had quite enough of this bullying.

'I think I'll hunt for Mrs Pillai's cottage.' Atiya thought to herself. She recalled that Gopal had once told her there was an old banyan tree in a corner of the garden, about thirty feet from the front door. Well, that would make it easy for her to locate the cottage. She had plenty of time to look for it.

She moved away from the bank and walked leisurely down to the old iron bridge that connected the forested edge of the sanctuary to the tiny tiled cottages on the other side of the river. The Ogre's voice receded as she neared the bridge and soon his voice was drowned out by the sounds of rushing water. She stopped in the middle of the bridge, peering down into the water as it swooshed and gushed below her. What a welcome song it sang, gurgling over the boulders. A couple of wagtails added pretty notes, with their tweets and whistles, and a redstart, sitting on a mossy stone at the waters' edge sang too. Peace at last! She watched a potter wasp carrying a green caterpillar away to its tiny mud nest. The hapless thing was already as good as 'dead meat' for the wasp larva. As soon as the larva hatched, it would feed on the caterpillar and finish its feast just about the time it was also ready to fly from its nest Nature was truly amazing!

She must have daydreamed on in a peaceful daze. Suddenly a dog barked and she could hear approaching voices. Better get off the bridge, she thought. If people recognized her, her father would soon know about her jungle escapades!

Three Kurumba tribals came out of the forest, with a scruffy looking mongrel walking in front of them. They talked among themselves, as they walked across the bridge. The men carried grimy cloth bags, full of forest produce. Probably a bee hive full of honey and dead bees or some berries and dioscorea tubers. It was fascinating how much these people could collect and eat from the jungles! City dwellers would freak out if they knew what sort of food was part of a Kurumba tribal's daily diet. Termite hill mushrooms, bracket fungi, perhaps the still unfurled leaves of young ferns, tubers of wild yam, wild amla fruits, tamarinds and even the sour green leaves of the tamarind tree. When wild fruits were in season there was jamun, mango, banana, even dates from the wild date palm. Atiya also knew of the thorny bamboo that grew in abundance in these jungles. Once in about thirty years, this particular species of bamboo would fruit and seed. Then it was truly party time for the Kurumbas! Entire families would go into the forest and collect as much bamboo seed—they looked like tiny grains of rice—as possible. They'd return home and the women would cook the seed to make a wonderful dish that they would eat for days together. Atiya had never tasted it, but heard that it was delicious stuff.

She waited till the men were well out of sight before she came out from behind a thick clump of bamboo, and on to the road again. She let them walk on and when the road took a turn and they had disappeared around it, she walked on following them at a slow pace. Soon she came to a fork and taking the right one, she passed the last bus stop sign. She realized it wouldn't be long before she was walking past the Ogre's cottage, this time from the front of the house. But Gopal and Mrs Pillai's cottage interested her more. Now, where was the old banyan tree? She walked on quite a way, and suddenly, there it was!

A huge banyan tree, its strong aerial roots firmly in the ground around the main trunk, its many horizontal old branches forming a wonderful shady canopy for a great seating area under it, in one corner of Gopal Pillai's front garden. Almost at once, she called it the Grandfather Banyan! It seemed to have a personality already and she decided to lie under it and take a nap. No one was about, and no one was likely to come by either. The Kurumbas were by now, far, far away. Peace descended on her and the old banyan, its low branches surrounding her in green leafy security. She took out her scarf, folded it to form a tiny pillow under her head and shut her eyes. Vaguely she heard the gushing of the river, and the birds twittering. Everything seemed to be taking an afternoon nap. Soon she too, was asleep.

Atiya slept fitfully. The Ogre's angry face kept popping up in her dreams. His eyes glared like two fiery balls and half his teeth were missing. And he was hideous! He kept spitting and hissing at Atiya like a demon. He shook a bamboo stick at her, trying to hit her with it, screaming wildly all the time. It was an awful nightmare! Finally he got a grip of her and the next thing she knew, she was yanked up and thrown into a bottomless well. Down, down, down . . . Her cries for help fell on deaf ears. All she could hear was the desperate echo of her own voice. She kept falling, falling, when all of a sudden, she heard a new sound. It was music! It came from the end of the tunnel. Aah! The Gates of Heaven, she realized. As she floated closer, the music grew louder, more angelic, more ethereal. It enveloped her completely. Its power and charm were captivating and it cast her under its spell. The music grew ever louder and finally she woke. She blinked, the strong sunlight searing through the canopy above her. And still she heard the music.

It was the flute!

Tiny flute notes floated across to her as she lay there mesmerized. Each note rang out, clear as a bell, light as a wisp of cloud, soft as a feather. It sounded like nothing she had ever heard before. She dared not move for fear the music would stop. Finally, the last notes died away and the sound of the jungle took over again.

Was it her imagination? No, there it was again!

She sat up. Now wide awake. It was the sound of her beloved flute. Someone very close by was playing it!

Atiya hurriedly stuffed her scarf into her backpack, clamped her cap on her head and hobbled unevenly and as fast she could out of the Pillai garden and down the mud track towards the sound. She *must* locate the flute player before the music stopped again! Who could it be?

She walked down the road as quick as she could, following the sound. There were tiled cottages on both sides of the road here and though she saw no one, the flute notes wafted out to her sensitive ears only too clearly. Like a lure, it pulled her ever closer. A pretty tiled cottage came into view. This one was a little distant from the rest. She could hear the reedy melody come from around the side of the house. Hesitantly she walked on, looking for someone, anyone, to give her directions. When she came around the eastern wall of the house, suddenly and much too late, she realized where she was.

There at the end of the green patch of grass and in his usual place, sat the Ogre in his armchair. In his hands he lightly held a long, beautifully carved, bamboo flute. His dark glasses on his nose, his fingers skimmed the top of the flute, as he played effortlessly, blowing into the instrument. He swayed gently and in rhythm to the fabulous music he played. Atiya stood transfixed, immersed completely. She never noticed the young woman come out of the back door with a tray in her hands——It was the saint!

The woman saw her first. She waited till the music came to an end. Then, with ease and a friendly smile, she beckoned. Atiya went silently forward. 'Come,' the woman's expression seemed to suggest.

Atiya walked up to the woman, and with her hands folded in greeting, she mimed the word. 'Namaste!' Atiya said in a whisper.

Once again, the woman smiled, folding her hands too in greeting as well, 'Who are you?' she asked her softly, as the music began again. 'And where are you from?'

Atiya told her, in whispered words. It was almost as if she hated breaking the spell of the music they could both hear. 'I'm Atiya Sardare. I live with my father at the forest lodge. Y . . . your father's music!' she said, and looked at the Ogre with a mixture of fear and fascination. 'It's beautiful!'

Atiya looked inquisitively at the young woman. She was thin, short and darker than the old man. She must have been about thirty. Her hair was pinned up into a bun and she'd tucked two thinly carved bamboo sticks the top. Now that Atiya got a closer look at her, she figured out that the young woman was a local Kurumba. Her huge eyes were black—her pupils enormous. Her eyelashes were long and she walked barefoot. Her plain red and yellow lungi was handwoven. She was extraordinarily beautiful. Atiya realized that she even *looked* like an angel.

The old man, oblivious of Atiya's sudden appearance, continued to play. Engrossed in his flute and the light windy notes he produced, the Ogre played on. Tune after tune, rising and falling, soft and gentle, loud and forceful, as he breathed into his instrument. The melodies were haunting, the double notes trilled up and down, filling the jungle with bubbly warbles. Sounds that made Atiya think of gurgling water rushing between crevices in the riverbanks and disappearing into them, only to reappear again, further downstream. She visualized images of Kurumba tribals dancing and celebrating, hunting and fishing, storytelling and caring for their young ones, living in the forest and dancing around a campfire . . .

The music he played brought him to life too. Atiya marvelled at his dexterity. She was completely under his spell, hypnotized and unable to think or speak! Within the short time he played his flute Atiya discovered to her surprise that the Ogre had transformed himself from a horrid evil old crank into a benevolent god of music! Finally there were no more notes to play, and the Ogre put his flute gently down on his lap. Atiya hadn't moved all through his playing. She wished he wouldn't stop.

But almost at once, the old man coughed and turned his head to face the young woman and Atiya.

'Mishora?' he called to the young tribal woman. The woman quickly took three steps forward and gently touched the old man's' knee. 'Yes, Papa?' she said, peering into his face.

His head bent a little to one side, as if he was listening for something, 'Is there someone here with us?'

Atiya froze in terror!

'Yes, Papa!' she heard Mishora reply.

Feeling a tug on her arm, she heard Mishora say, 'You have to meet our guest, Papa!' She pulled Atiya by the hand, up to the Ogre. She placed Atiya's hand gently in the old man's gnarled fingers.

Atiya flinched for a fleeting second, but decided the Ogre had to be given a second chance. Only someone very talented and very sensitive could have played the flute as well and with such ease as he had. The old man felt her palm with a very light but firm touch of his fingertips—as if he were reading Braille. At last he spoke. 'This hand belongs to someone I do not know,' said the Ogre, speaking in English. He looked puzzled.

'Yes, indeed, Papa!' said Mishora. 'This is Atiya, the daughter of forest ranger, Ram Deva Sardare.'

'Ah, yes!' said the Ogre, in a distant whisper. 'Sardare, the man whose wife left to dance on stage . . . yes?' Mishora grimaced in silence, a pained expression on her face.

'Papa does not know how to be polite sometimes,' she said to Atiya, as if apologizing for the old man's' bluntness, 'But I know he was very fond of your parents. There was a time when they knew each other well!'

Atiya hadn't spoken until then. She was mesmerized by the Ogre. So *he* was the player of the haunting flute melodies she had heard in the jungle that day with Gopal! What a surprise! She stepped closer to the old man.

'Good afternoon, Uncle,' she greeted him softly. 'I was walking in the jungle on the other side of the river, when I heard you play the flute . . .' her voice trailed off. Would this man take a nasty swipe at her, like the Ogre he had been in her dream? Somehow, the power of his music had given her courage. She took another breath and began again. 'You make it sound like heavenly music!' she said in an impetuous rush.

Mishora reached out and touched Atiya's hand. The young woman, Atiya noticed, had the kindest of smiles and her eyes were moist, full of emotion. Mishora nodded her head in silent agreement. 'Yes, that's the right word,' she nodded again, 'He plays the flute like no one else I know!'

The Ogre sat still and silent. The flute lay idly in his lap, his fingers gently feeling the bamboo instrument as if it were alive. His smile became a little friendly. He turned in Atiya's direction, letting her hand go. 'You liked the music?' he asked her. Atiya noticed his smile was fixed, but tone of his voice was not Ogre-like at all. He even had all his teeth in place, there were none missing. He wasn't hideous looking, like the evil man in her horrid nightmare. This old man only had the most wrinkled face she'd ever seen. He looked like he was a hundred-years-old!

'Yes, I think you play beautifully!' Atiya replied, looking at him. Quickly, she sat down, cross-legged, on the grass, at his feet. 'Months ago I had heard the flute in the jungle.' She said, looking up at him in awe. Then in a rush added, 'But I never knew it was you who played it!'

Mishora served some juice and then rushed back into the cottage and came out with a third glass for herself. She joined her father and Atiya, sitting like her, at his feet. 'Papa, tell her about your music!' Mishora pleaded. 'I think Atiya wants to know more about you and the music you play!'

'Yes, that's true!' Atiya said with hardly contained excitement. 'When did you learn to play the flute? What music were you playing now?'

The old man leaned back in his chair, the smile still playing at the corner of his mouth. Atiya wished she could see his eyes, but they were hidden behind his dark glasses. A gradual change of expression from happy to pensive came over the man's features. Atiya waited patiently. She had all the time in the world now that he wasn't an ogre any more!

'Ah, well!' said the old man, with a wave of his hand, 'Where should I begin?'

Mishora laughed, and clapped her hands. 'From when you came here to work?'

'Ah, yes!' began the old man. His wrinkles vanished, as he began to speak. 'I came to work with the local tribals many, many years ago . . .I was about twenty-five-years-old.' He coughed. His thin shoulders heaving uncomfortably. 'The anthropology department posted me here to work with the Kurumbas—to find out more about their customs, norms and traditions.'

Atiya and Mishora smiled at each other, and waited for him to continue. Atiya knew this was going to be a long story, but she was fascinated by the old man and his daughter and had no wish to miss a single word.

It was a spellbinding story! He described the tiny Kurumba village with its small tribal community, 'There were many old and wise men and women. And there was the younger generation. Many curious customs and traditions of this small, close knit community fascinated me. I documented them meticulously over the first five years that I spent with them.' His hands still played ever so gently with the bamboo flute, almost as if he were caressing the head of an infant. 'There were special ceremonies when a baby was born, or at a funeral,' he continued. 'Their traditional foods and medicines, even their folk tales, which I had actually heard first hand from a grand old lady—one of the oldest members of the Kurumba community. I spent many, many months writing down everything, word for word, just as the

Wise Old Granny, as I had by then named her, had actually told me.'

'Many of his research papers were printed in international research books,' Mishora added proudly. 'Pretty soon, he had become a famous author of several books on the Kurumbas. In south India he was often called "Learned Man of the Kurumbas". People would come from very far, often from overseas, just to listen to Papa, and hear about his experiences with the Kurumbas of the south.'

The old man shrugged and coughed again, holding a hand to his chest as he did so. Atiya realized he was not very fit, he kept coughing and the beautiful hands that played the flute so mystically, now shook feebly in his lap as he listened to his daughter. He must be ill.

'My work with the Kurumbas became the best years of my life,' said the old man. 'I had worked with them for at least twenty years. Then, one summer, I fell sick. They told me later that I was very ill and had almost lost my life. Thanks to one Kurumba woman, however, I survived. That was Misha. She looked after me with such love and care. So immersed was I in my research all through those twenty years, that until then I hadn't even noticed her as a person. Of course, in those first few years she was still much like a child herself.' His voice faded away, lost in thought.

Again Mishora laughed and interrupted her father. 'Misha, you may have guessed, was my mother,' she told Atiya with pride. 'After she helped Papa get better, he asked her to marry him. The other Kurumbas were very happy for them both, but Papa's family in Chennai was upset and never forgave him for his decision.'

'However, I wasn't upset. Mama was the most precious gift God could have given me,' said the old man, patting Mishora on her mop of thick black hair. No one was happier than we were, especially when Mishora was born.' Here, Mishora chuckled, her eyes as bright as two black diamonds.

'That's when he began to play the flute,' said Mishora. 'My Kurumba grandfather gave Papa a bamboo flute as a gift the year of my birth. And pretty soon Papa was playing lovely music. He used to play his flute at night when it was time for me to sleep.'

'That was,' said the old man, 'when I began to realize that an entire segment of the Kurumba lifestyle and customs was missing from my research work. It was in the field of music. I decided to go into a new branch of research—Kurumba music and instruments.'

Atiya sat open-mouthed in awe. This old man—she didn't even know his name yet—had led a fascinating life.

'Now, I wanted to learn the intricacies of the flute, its various types, traditional folk tunes, music for special occasions, even the lyrics,' the old man told her, 'I knew I had only just touched the tip of the iceberg. And, like with everything else, I wanted to learn all I could about the flute. Every little tribal melody, tune, folk song, perhaps even religious songs, that is if they had them! 'Don't forget, good tape recorders were not available at that time. In any case, they could never reproduce the sounds of the flute as they sounded when you heard the instrument live in the jungle. So,' he snapped his fingers in the air, grinning widely, 'I set to work. It took me several years to get to where I am now. Misha passed away suddenly one winter and I couldn't play for a year after that. Mishora was my only solace. She studied in the village school and we lived in a tiny house there. Many years passed . . .' Suddenly his voice trailed away, and he sighed deeply. Atiya realized that he couldn't get the words out of his mouth.

'And then, soon after Papa's seventieth birthday, he wasn't feeling too good. We went to the doctor in Mysore. They told us that Papa,' here Mishora gulped and her eyes became moist, 'has a degenerating disease. It would affect first, his sight and then gradually spread to the other organs in his body. They told us he has only a few more months to live . . .' and the tears poured silently down her cheeks.

Atiya squirmed. The poor Ogre. She cried silent tears in her heart for this old man. Surely this wasn't true? But she only had to see him with his dark glasses, to realize he had probably become blind already. No wonder he was so frustrated and angry all the time. And no wonder that Mishora was so infinitely patient and caring for her father. She knew she would soon be losing him forever. What about the haunting melodies, the flute notes, the ethereal tunes or the very sound of the flute? They too would be gone forever when the old man died.

'No, no!' Atiya replied sadly, 'Why do you live here, so far from the hospital? Perhaps if you were closer, Uncle would get better again?'

Both father and daughter shook their heads sadly. 'No thank you,' said the Ogre with finality. 'I just wanted to be in my own little green garden and enjoy playing the flute here, till I cannot do so, any more!'

'And I want him to be happy, wherever it might be . . .' added Mishora. She froze in mid-smile and the old man bent his head in renewed despair and frustration. He looked so low that Atiya jumped up impetuously, and grabbed his hand again. She pressed it lightly and said in a hurry, 'Don't give up playing, Uncle. You play so well!' She sighed deeply. 'I wish . . .'

The Ogre turned again, in her direction. 'What is it you wish, my child?'

'Oh, I wish . . .I . . .Papa doesn't want me to learn to play the flute!' Atiya told them in a rush.

Mishora came to her side quickly and touched her lightly on her arm.

'Why?' she asked. It was obvious that Atiya yearned to play the flute.

'My mother left Papa to dance on stage, remember?' Atiya explained, 'He is afraid I will go away too, once I learn to play well enough. He thinks I will go back to the city and forget all about him, like my mother.'

'You poor, poor thing!' Mishora gave her a warm consoling hug. Suddenly, she clapped her hands. She had hit upon an idea! Would it work? 'Papa, could we do something about that?'

The Ogre looked in Mishora's direction, expressionless. Then he smiled slowly and nodded. 'Hmm!' he said, quietly, 'Yes! We could solve that problem, I think. Mishora?'

But Mishora was already running indoors. Seconds later she was back. In her hands and holding it aloft in triumph, was a replica of the Ogre's bamboo flute. She placed it gently in Atiya's hands and the girl squealed with delight. He turned to smile at her. Atiya's Ogre was truly a god of music!

'If you are really keen to learn,' she heard the old man say, 'I will be happy to teach you, my child. We can begin lessons as soon as you want—no one needs to know. Perhaps when you're an expert your father will think differently.'

Atiya let out another whoop of joy, hugged Mishora and impetuously touched the old man's shoulder. 'Thank you, thank you!' was all she could say.

As if to emphasize the importance of the moment, the clock in the cottage rang out four times and Atiya jumped. It was time to get home.

'I'll be here at ten tomorrow morning. And thank you again!' Quickly Atiya hugged them both and walked as fast as her legs allowed her to. She waved at the corner of the house and reached the bus stop just as the old jalopy creaked and groaned down the road towards her. The driver crossed the bridge and turned the bus around, stopping at the bus stop directly in front of her. He was new, he didn't recognize her. She breathed easy.

Getting off at her own village, Atiya sailed on air as

she walked up her driveway. Her head buzzed with her secret. Her father must not find out that she was learning to play the flute! At least, not for the moment.

Was her dream finally going to come true?

RANGAPPA

The sun was up early next morning, almost as if it knew Atiya was about to embark on a new phase in her life. She gobbled up her breakfast and told Angasammy she would be home late. He packed the usual generous lunch in a hamper for her. The days were getting hotter, but there was a growing humidity in the air. The monsoon clouds were building up more each day. Atiya knew the rains would soon be here.

Atiya got into the bus. Two passengers behind her talked loudly. They were discussing Rangappa, the rogue elephant's latest escapades on the sanctuary edge. The animal had become quite a menace in the region. Some were demanding that it be shot before it harmed more people. 'Already,' one man said to the other, 'he has nine deaths on his record. Ranger Sardare will soon have to do something about that!' They were discussing Rangappa as if he was an evil criminal.

Atiya had quite forgotten the story of the trampled German photographer. Now she recalled the episode again. Kronhaage was a great man with a fabulous talent for wildlife photography. Why do we humans always think we can reason things out better than the animals who share the earth with us? If Kronhaage had given some more space to Rangappa; if he had not invaded it with total disrespect for the animal, things could have been different.

The new driver hooted as the bus rumbled round a sharp corner and began to climb a steep hill. They reached the top shuddering along and suddenly, there on the top edge of the road, Atiya saw—Rangappa! At the same time everyone else in the bus saw the rogue elephant. A collective cry of fear rose from the passengers. The driver jammed his brakes hard. The bus ground to a halt, just thirty feet away from the animal.

A deadly silence filled the bus, amidst whispered words of 'Rangappa', '*Aanay*', 'dangerous animal'. Atiya held her breath, watching the elephant—what would the animal do now? The driver could hardly take the bus down quickly in reverse on such a steep slope. The elephant couldn't walk up the steep bank on either side of the road at this point. The animal had only one option. Walk back up and away from the bus, along the road until it found a way back into the safety of the jungle on the side of the road, at a point where he could do so with ease.

Atiya realized the new driver was petrified, quite unused to dealing with this kind of emergency. Terrified, he tried to frighten away the animal. He revved his engine and hooted his horn twice, making Rangappa furious. The elephant mock charged once, then backed off, his ears flapping in fury, his front feet and trunk stirring up the mud on the roadside in a mass of brown dust. The driver revved up some more and hooted again. Rangappa trumpeted like the truly infuriated elephant that he now was. Suddenly they heard the most terrifying sound from the animal's throat. A deep, menacing, stupefying rumble that kept on and on and on! No sound they had heard was as terrifying as this one! Everyone knew they were seconds from disaster.

Atiya thought fast. She got up quickly and walked up to the driver.

'Sshhhhshhhh!' she whispered to him, her finger on her lips, 'Don't upset him, please! Just switch your engine off and don't scare him any more.' Then turning to the passengers in the bus, she said as calmly as she could, 'Please, be silent. Let the animal go in peace. We must remain silent, please!'

By now most of the passengers recognized her. 'Ranger Sardare's daughter,' one young man said quietly, 'She knows about such things. We should listen to her.' Quickly, the driver switched off his engine, and pulled up the handbrake.

Atiya breathed a sigh of relief when she saw how fast the people in the bus sat down. No one said a word. They trusted her. All of them had their eyes on Rangappa, who was still rumbling madly at them. His trunk waved around, lashing at whatever was within grasp. He pulled off branches and leaves, tufts of grass and bits of sticks and hurled them towards the bus, growling deep in his throat.

The passengers sat in terrified silence. Gradually, very gradually, the enraged animal calmed down, the rumbles stopped and then, as quickly as he had appeared, he turned on his heels. In as dignified a manner as possible, he walked away from the bus. The driver gave him ten minutes more to find his way off the road. Then he started up his engine and drove up the hill. Looking down on their left, they saw that Rangappa had made a quiet and peaceful exit. A collective sigh of relief, a few low chuckles and the group sat back to enjoy the rest of the ride.

The last stop soon appeared and Atiya hopped off. The driver waved goodbye with a 'thank you' in Tamil, and she waved back. 'See you later!' she said, as she walked down the road towards the cottages.

It had already drizzled here, she noticed. The raindrops still glinted on the mud track as she walked along. A pair of grey hornbills squealed as they flew overhead, but Atiya's mind was apprehensive and alert. She was so focussed on this morning's first flute lesson—she knew she wanted to try her best. Every nerve in her body was awake and jangling. She was worried she would do something stupid or dumb and madden the Ogre at their first lesson together.

A tiny thought came into her head. The resemblance between the Ogre and Rangappa. Crazy though it was, it was striking. Both were angry, frustrated and short-tempered. Both suffered from some grievous injury or illness, and both were very lonely. Outcasts, in a strange way, in their own worlds.

Little did Atiya know that she held the key to opening those worlds—for both the Ogre and the elephant.

That key would come her way soon.

FIRST LESSON

Atiya walked through the front door of the Ogre's cottage, apprehensive. Would he be patient with her, or would he throw his usual tantrums? She must be positive. She was going to begin flute lessons. It was going to be a great experience. She must try to come here as often as she could and learn as quickly as possible. For a while, no one other than Mishora and the Ogre must know of this venture. If the news did get out, her father would hear of it and he might be upset with her. It was going to be difficult to keep it a secret from him, but for a while she must. For the moment, she had another goal as well. She was going to try very hard to make the lessons fun for the Ogre, too. After all, he had offered to teach her the flute. In return, she was going to strive to help him enjoy his last few months of life, just as she knew Mishora had made up her mind to do, too.

That was going to be the difficult part. For the Ogre—and she must give him another name, he wasn't an Ogre at all—had the shortest temper she'd seen in anyone. How was she going to keep him from blowing his top, like an old volcano, every five minutes?

Mishora opened the thick jackwood door almost immediately after Atiya knocked. SHIVAN, said the brass plaque above the knocker.

'Hi, Mishora!' Atiya greeted her, with an excited hug. 'Hello, Uncle!' she called out. There was no reply. 'Where's your father?' She raised her eyebrows enquiringly at Mishora who shook her head and gave her gorgeous smile.

'Not to worry!' she said, 'He's waiting impatiently for you, in the garden. Go, go!' and she shooed Atiya out through the living room towards the back garden.

'Hello, Uncle!' Atiya called out again, as she walked up to him, across the green grass. Atiya picked up his hand, as it lay listless on his lap, but he snapped at her, and she jumped in fright. Had he become the Ogre again, after all?

'Don't touch me!' he yelled. 'You are ten minutes late. I know the time. That's not going to do at all!'

Mishora heard him from the door and called out to him, 'Papa, Oh, Papa. Give Atiya some time. She doesn't come here by car, you know. She had a bus to catch, so if the driver is late, well, she'll be late, too. Besides, she cannot walk like you and me. She has a bad leg . . .'

Uncle Shivan was silent a moment. Then he yelled again, 'What do you mean, "a bad leg"?' he asked.

Atiya, who was tongue-tied during this exchange, turned to the old man. 'I had polio as a child,' she told him standing quietly beside his chair, 'One of my legs is shorter and weaker than the other.'

'Hmmph!' grumbled the old man in an undertone. What was he muttering to himself? Did he seem a little apologetic? But no, he wasn't sorry. Almost immediately he spoke again, this time clearly and firmly. 'I don't care about your legs, got that? Be here on time, otherwise, no lesson! Is that clear?'

'Yes, Uncle!' Atiya replied quietly again. She had come here with a goal—nothing was going to shake her off, nothing short of an earthquake!

'Hmmmph!' said the old man a second time. Her handicap was never mentioned by any of them again.

In a trice, his voice changed. Now he spoke in a quiet, patient tone, the sort a wise old teacher would use on an attentive pupil! 'Right! Let's begin!' He picked up his flute, and said, 'Have you got your flute? The bamboo one?'

Atiya nodded silently, but realized he couldn't see her, so she spoke, 'Yes, I do. I have it in my hands.'

'Right. Now place your fingers over the holes, like this . . .' And he showed her how to cover each hole. First, the four top holes with the fingers of her left hand, then the lower four with the fingers of her right hand. 'You hold your flute with the thumbs of each hand, sliding them back and forth under the instrument, like this . . .' Again he showed her how to use her thumbs to balance the flute as he blew into the top blowhole of his own instrument.

Atiya followed every move with concentration. Mishora, who was watching from the kitchen window, smiled to herself. Atiya had the determination of a young fiend, the young woman decided. She had a gut feeling that there were going to be horrific fireworks between these two, her dear cranky old father and this impetuous young girl. Deep in her heart, she hoped that her sad and frustrated father would finally have something to look forward to again, even if he was given only a short while more to live. 'Oh, dear god, let there please be happiness in this home again!' she prayed fervently. As she scrubbed away at the dishes, she saw the rays of early morning sunlight shine down through the trees on their bent heads, one almost bald, the other, smaller and black as shining coal.

Already, the first few sounds of the flute came wafting in through her kitchen window. It was her father playing a short tune. A slow piece, with long, held notes, all the way up and then down the scale. He played it once, and then, he began again. Quite suddenly, Mishora could hear another tinnier sound. Atiya was following the old man's notes, exactly the same pitch, note by note, and to exactly the same length of time.

Each time the old man stopped, Atiya would stop too. A long discussion followed. Mishora knew her father was explaining how to breathe through the flute, how to hold the note, make warbles, like the trilling of a bird and so many more of the finer points of playing this instrument. Atiya said little. She listened, her black eyes opened wide, listening and nodding, trying to take in everything he said.

When, Mishora finally, took out glasses of juice to the two at the end of the garden, they were sitting quietly. It must have been at least two hours and her father had only just stopped talking. Suddenly, he looked exhausted.

Atiya helped Mishora with the plate of biscuits.

'Oh, Papa, are you tired, then?' Mishora asked the old man. But the Ogre lay peacefully in his chair, his head back, and a tiny smile playing on his lips.

'No, no!' he told them, waving his arms in dismissal. 'I think we may just have a budding musician here.'

Atiya clapped her hands in delight. Had she heard right?

'I think he's just trying to be polite, for a change.' Mishora said, teasing her, watching Atiya's grin disappear as quick as it had come.

'Quite right!' said the old man, short and curt, all of a sudden. 'You may have the talent, but that's nothing to go by. Only if you practise well and thoroughly and learn about the intricacies of this instrument, yes! Only then will I say you have the makings of a true musician,' said the Ogre, a finger wagging menacingly at her, and the grin nowhere to be seen.

Atiya listened to his words; she wanted so much to give him a fiery retort. Then she remembered her goal and swallowed her words humbly. 'I must listen to him, raving or angry, calm or kind. He cannot be an ogre and his words are wise,' she told herself again, determined to do her best.

'Yes, Uncle,' she answered his outburst with a calm maturity far beyond her years, 'I'll try my best to do as you say. There's only one thing I beg of you?'

'What's that?' the old man leaned forward in his chair, curiosity getting the upper hand, and forgetting his grumpiness for a while.

'Please do not tell anyone about our lessons,' begged Atiya, 'If my father hears of it, he . . .!'

'Ahaaa!' said Mishora and her father together, 'We do not meet any one, so who can we tell?'

'What about your neighbours, here?' Atiya asked.

'No one lives here,' Mishora replied for both of them. 'There is only Mrs Pillai, who lives down the road in one of the first tiled cottages—too far from here! Anyway, she's in Chennai, right now.' And they forgot about the matter almost at once. Atiya still had to fix up times for future lessons.

'Papa is returning from Mysore tonight,' she told them, 'I shall be. able to come only at eleven every weekday during my holidays. Once he leaves for work, I can catch the bus to this village. On Papa's day off, Sunday, I cannot come.'

They decided that eleven o'clock would be fine, and she could stay for lunch if she wished. 'That's no trouble for me,' said Mishora cheerfully, 'We'll be glad for the company!' Atiya noticed that the Ogre didn't make a comment. He just grunted. 'Hummph!' he said, with a frown on his face.

They heard the bus coming soon after that; it was about lunch time. Mishora asked her to have lunch with them, but Atiya was a little nervous. What if her father came back early and found her out? She could not afford to be caught now, just after she'd discovered her precious, though grumpy flute player and actually begun flute lessons! No way.

Mishora walked back with her to the bus stop, listening to Atiya's story about her bus trip that morning. She was describing Rangappa, his scary tantrums and his distaste for human beings.

'I think I can see why the elephant is so bad-tempered,' Mishora said with sympathy, 'People probably do not leave him in peace. The jungles are getting smaller all the time, less wild and there are more and more of us around. How can the poor beast stay aloof, when there are so many "invasions" into his private space?'

Atiya looked at Mishora, seeing this young woman in a new light. Mishora understood the animal completely. And she, Atiya, had found another kindred spirit! Almost double her age, almost a surrogate mother, and yet, able to come to Atiya's level of understanding instinctively. Mishora was turning out to be another close friend.

TWO OF A KIND

Atiya was early for lessons each day of the remaining vacations. Papa never found out. Much as she would have loved to borrow the flute and take it home with her, there was no point in doing so, for Papa would have heard her play it—that would have been no good at all.

She looked forward to her lessons so eagerly that the days and weeks flew by. Finally one Friday, at the end of May, she looked up her calendar to discover that there was just a week before village school reopened. Seven days. After that, she knew it would be tough to get away and her lessons would have to be reduced to just one per week, on Saturdays. That would be the day when Papa would be at work and she was free to get away for a couple of hours. When she got to the Shivans' cottage that Friday morning, her heart was heavy, and Mishora sensed it at once.

'What's the matter?' she asked as soon as Atiya walked in through the door.

'School reopens in a week,' Atiya told her, grimacing. 'I will only be able to come on Saturdays.'

Mishora looked over her shoulder at her father sitting outside in the back garden. He was waiting for his pupil to arrive. 'Look at Papa,' Mishora said, her eyes enormous and full of pride, 'He's been waiting patiently for you. I don't know how he'll take your news. He's beginning to look forward to your visits so much!'

Atiya nodded. True. It hadn't always been like this. The atmosphere in the tiny cottage, since her first lesson had almost imperceptibly, but very gradually changed.

The first few days were the worst. Each day as she approached their home, she could hear the Ogre yelling angrily, shouting orders, complaining, whining and behaving like his usual self—horrible, mean and nasty. Each time, she'd hear Mishora's voice, placating, cajoling, coaxing and caring. Atiya admired this woman for her patience and her love for the Ogre. How much she loved her father, Atiya marvelled! Mishora would forgive him always. His impatience and rudeness were only because he couldn't get used to his blindness and the slow but sure degeneration of his body, she would tell Atiya. An infinite acceptance for her dear ailing father was borne of a deep and boundless love and admiration. Mishora truly was an angel.

Atiya's first few classes were the worst. Every little while, the old man would hit his forehead in despair, and shout at her. He was rude, impatient and cold-hearted, and Atiya was often on the verge of telling him so. How dare he scream at her! Why should she listen to his raving at all? She didn't have to tolerate it. But she quickly learnt that a loud retort would only anger him more. And she was determined to have her flute lessons, no matter what tantrums she had to stomach. So each time he yelled, Atiya would take a deep breath, get her wits together and begin playing again.

On one occasion, a fortnight after she'd begun lessons, the Ogre heard her practise a finger exercise over and over. Each time she'd hesitate at one point and end up blowing the wrong note. Finally, he exploded. 'Aaaah!'

he screamed, clamping his ears shut with both his hands, 'You are useless! Don't even try it. You cannot play a decent tune! Your fingers are iron rods, not fingers at all! Aaaagh!' And he waved his arms at her, as if to say 'Go! Get out of my sight!' Atiya sat down, shattered and silent. She couldn't move. An awful silence filled the air. She wanted to cry aloud in despair. She put down the flute and picked herself off the grass in slow motion, terrified of the thought that she would never have another chance at playing the flute any more. It was too depressing to think about. She dared not say a word. He was ready to strangle her, he looked so wild! She stared at him, trying hard to think of something to soften him, but she couldn't.

Suddenly, they both heard a sharp *crack*!

Atiya and the Ogre turned towards the opposite bank, from where the sound had come. Standing there was a large and lone elephant. Atiya recognized him at once. How long had he been standing there?

'Rangappa!' she gasped aloud.

The Ogre turned to her. The frown had disappeared. His expression was now one of passive, mild interest. 'The rogue elephant?' he murmured.

'Yes, Ogre Uncle!' Atiya replied under her breath.

In her excitement she hadn't realized what she'd just called him. The Ogre, however, had heard it clearly. He didn't say a word. 'Rogue elephant?' he asked again, eyebrows raised.

'Yes, he's mean and nasty and doesn't like people,' Atiya informed him quietly. All at once she recalled the similarity between the Ogre and this elephant. This was the chance she'd been waiting for! 'He's probably ill, too,' she added, as if it was an afterthought.

'Why do you say that?' The old man was genuinely interested to know more about this animal. He seemed to have quite forgotten the outburst over her rotten playing. In fact, the flute lay in his lap and he was leaning forward, as if waiting eagerly for her to speak.

'My father tells me Rangappa's been thrown out of his herd. He's Probably unwell, that's why he's so bad tempered,' Atiya explained.

'Unwell?' said the Ogre.

'Perhaps Rangappa ventured too often into some one's sugarcane farm. Perhaps the farmer tried to poison him, or injure him, or even to shoot him dead. Or perhaps he's just very, very old . . . who knows?' Atiya said softly, as she watched the elephant lift its trunk and smell them from across the bank. Her father had often told her that these mighty animals couldn't see too well, but they had a very keen hearing and sense of smell. They also had very good memories.

Rangappa was aware of the human beings on the opposite bank. He stood very still and flapped his ears, trying to pick up the sound of their voices. Sixty years of experience seemed to have taught him to be wary of human beings. So far, they had only meant trouble. He began to thrash about, breaking some more branches for extra effect.

Atiya watched the elephant for a while. The Ogre, she noted with subconscious interest, kept asking her questions about him. As if the animal, somehow interested him. And, biggest surprise of all, he seemed to have forgotten his anger altogether. What a welcome change from the yelling and shouting he'd been up to earlier. Atiya relieved, decided to try and keep him interested in the animal and its behaviour. She'd give the flute a miss for the rest of the day. She came closer to his chair and sat down at his feet again. This time she faced the opposite bank, and hesitatingly at first, she began to describe the rogue elephant to the Ogre.

'Rangappa is very tall, Uncle,' she began slowly. 'He has two very long tusks—about two feet long. One is a little thinner than the other. That's how the rangers can identify him. His head has a big bulge on the top, probably where his brain is and his face, especially near his eyes, is wrinkly and wise . . .' She stopped to look at the Ogre. He was listening quietly.

'Do you think he's clever, or is he just a big, dumb animal?' he asked, his head turned towards the other bank with his ear cupped as if listening for sounds of the animal.

Atiya smiled. Hmmm. He *was* interested! She heaved a sigh of relief, wanting desperately to giggle. What a crazy situation she was in. Here she was, describing one rogue elephant to another. 'I wonder if they see something common in each other,' she thought to herself, trying hard to keep a straight face.

'I think he's very clever. In fact, I think Rangappa is shrewd,' Atiya told the Ogre quietly. She was getting the beginnings of an idea. Would it work? She decided, impetuously to try it. 'He craves attention,' Atiya told the Ogre, 'And he knows he is unable to get it from his own kind. So, he turns to throwing weird fits, breaking branches, thrashing his trunk against the trees and terrifying human beings.'

'Humph! Yes, continue . . .?' said the Ogre, hand still cupped for elephant noises from the other bank. He was and she knew it, actually listening to her. Atiya was thankful he couldn't see her smile. 'Well, this behaviour doesn't help him at all, does it?' She continued, 'It just upsets people. If he carries on this way, pretty soon everyone will want to see him dead.'

'You think so?' asked the Ogre, now turning to face her. 'Is there a way to make him change then?'

Atiya nodded, her smile wide now. 'Yes, I think so. We have to show him that we do care and that we'd love to help him, but—first he must be calmer and better behaved!'

'How does one teach him that?' asked the Ogre. His face was pensive and she saw he had leaned back in his armchair, his head bent a little.

'We have to teach him to trust us again,' Atiya said, 'My father once told me that in life, everything is a symbiosis, an inter-dependency that is constant and needed for life to be meaningful. We must teach him that he needs us as much as we need him.'

The Ogre's hands lay still in his lap. He was suddenly very quiet. Atiya watched him from the corner of her eye. Had he fallen asleep, or was he thinking? The elephant, on the other bank seemed to be doing much the same thing!

Rangappa, too, was standing still, his ears gently

flapping, as he heard her calm sing-song voice. His trunk gently nibbled tufts of grass from the ground in front of him. Agitation and anger seemed to have disappeared. He looked much like any of the tame elephants in the elephant camp, just twenty kilometres away.

Watching him and then turning to the Ogre, Atiya began to get goosebumps. They were both now as calm as sleeping babes, peaceful and silent. She hadn't said or done anything very earth shattering, so why this sudden change in their behaviour?

Quick as lightning, she picked up her flute and began to blow into it. Very softly at first, then stronger, as she became more confident, she began to play the first few notes of a tribal tune the Ogre had taught her just a week before. And she didn't stop till the melody was done and the last notes flew away lightly on the first midday breeze. Even to her own ears, she thought she played the tune with sensitivity and feeling. It was a simple but haunting tune, full of trills and pretty little double notes and the words of the tribal melody seemed to have been invented for just this moment:

The Breeze blows my song through the ancient forest,
Hear it, my friend, oh hear it, then!
Casting a spell over all of us creatures . . .

Peace, it says, is a friend we all can share,
Join hands . . . and . . . catch the breeze!

The Ogre sat as still as a statue and as she played the last note, he lifted up his own flute and added two impromptu lines of music, like an answering song from the creatures of the forest. Atiya could actually hear bird calls, a wisp of breeze, the whirr of wings and even a cricket chirring in his melody!

'Oh, brilliant!' Atiya clapped her hands ecstatically. Someone laughed happily from behind them and there was Mishora, coming out to join them with the tray and glasses of juice. They picked up their glasses and silently watched Rangappa on the other bank raise his trunk, sniffing the human smell of them. He watched them, listening quietly for as long as it took them to sit and finish their glasses of juice, then at last he turned and just as quietly, he walked back away into his forest home.

In the months that followed, Atiya often recalled that awesome episode. It was almost a spiritual moment when the Ogre and Rangappa had stared silently and with mutual respect at each other. She would never forget the elephant standing like a statue as she played the tribal tune, as if he too loved every note he heard coming across the bank to his flapping ears! And strangest of all, she would never forget her flute master's comment as he bade her goodbye after that lesson.

'We'll see you next week, my child!' he said with the first gentle farewell wave he had allowed himself to give anyone for a very long time, 'And from now on please call me Ogre Uncle!'

Atiya had gasped in shock. Had she called him by her secret name for him at some point, she wondered in horror? But Ogre Uncle was grinning mischievously, and for the first time, she could see a wonderful sense of humour beneath that cold, hard, cranky exterior. She vowed to herself that she would try everything in her power to get him to rediscover this joy of life—as soon as possible!

OGRE UNCLE IS ILL

The village school reopened. Within a week everyone was back in class. Atiya was thrilled to meet Mrs Pillai again. As luck would have it, Mrs Pillai was given responsibility of the tenth standard students that year. Atiya was skipping on air when she heard the news. She waited till the final bell to get news of Gopal.

When the last student had left the classroom, Atiya gathered her books together and went to Mrs Pillai.

The teacher was putting away her register and getting her things ready for next day's work. They hugged and Mrs Pillai held Atiya by the shoulders, peering into her grinning face.

'My dear,' she said, 'You're looking well and I think, yes,' squinting her eyes at Atiya, 'I think you've grown another four inches in the vacations!'

Atiya shrugged, but grinned happily, 'I've been having lots of exercise!'

'Really?' asked Naina Pillai, happy for this ambitious girl, 'Part of your physiotherapy, then?'

Atiya shook her head. 'Not really.' She didn't say more. Mrs Pillai left it at that. Today teenagers needed their space and she didn't want to impose on this girl. She knew it was a tough life for her, as it was, without a mother to share secrets with and a father who was more often than not, busy with his work and had little time to spare.

She recalled Ram Sardare and decided to switch the subject. 'How's your father—as busy as ever?'

This time Atiya nodded, 'As usual. He's been away and I've spent much of my holiday here.'

Mrs Pillai remembered something. 'Gopal gave me a letter for you,' she told Atiya. 'He's enjoying his time with his father—playing a lot of cricket. He's also joined the WWF and attended their wildlife camp in the Annamallais. I have a letter here, for you.' She ferreted in her purse, and fished out a bulky but rather crumpled envelope with Gopal's familiar writing on the cover. She handed it to Atiya.

Gopal had drawn green leafy trees along the edge of the envelope. 'Atiya S.' it said in dark green felt pen on the top. A yellow smiley sun splotched up one bright corner, a typical Gopal creation, she thought, grinning broadly. Mrs Pillai could not help but notice the girl's happy smile. Something had changed in this child while she had been away. She seemed more mature, calmer, less headstrong, or was it that she was simply just growing up? Naina couldn't put her finger on it, but there definitely was a change! Atiya had an air of confidence now. Her shiny black hair still longer, had almost overnight become very attractive indeed. Her skin was smooth and her cheeks were a lovely healthy pink. And her eyes, with those enormous long lashes! Where had she seen those before? Just recently, too. Ah, yes, At a dance recital, in Bangalore. Sarojini Sardare Jaithra, the Bharatnatyam dancer who had performed at a cultural do and was the chief artiste. Later, Naina had visited Ram Sardare's estranged wife backstage and noticed the resemblance to their daughter Atiya. It was striking! The same jet black hair, the same eyes, shape of face, even the lissome, remarkably feminine look. She wondered if Ram Sardare had met his wife in recent years. She was still as charming, good-looking and talented as she must have been so many years before, when they had first met. Ram himself—just as tall, handsome and gentlemanly as Naina remembered him in college. She sighed, lost in thought. Strange, the way fate turns out. Had she got to know him better so many years ago, perhaps her own life might just have turned to be out different too. Ah, well, no time to think of such things now.

She shrugged herself into the present again. Atiya was staring at her, a little confused with the thoughtful look on Naina Pillai's face.

'Are you staying at the Banyan Tree cottage again?' she asked Mrs Pillai, who nodded.

'It's a lovely tree, isn't it?' Naina said. They heard the last bus driving up to the village and Mrs Pillai got her things together at jet speed.

'I'll see you tomorrow,' she called out to Atiya in a rush, as she ran off to get the bus. 'I'm so glad to see you doing well. We'll talk again later.' And she was off.

Atiya walked slowly back home, Gopal's letter clutched in her hands. She tore the envelope open as soon as she got to her room. A photograph of Gopal fell to the ground. He looked quite striking with a stylish hair cut, and the faint beginnings of a moustache on his upper lip. He wore a green camouflage shirt. It made Atiya smile. The five sheets of thin paper in the envelope were covered with Gopal's scrawl. Untidy handwriting! There were dozens of tiny sketches, a couple of newspaper cuttings, even a complete magazine article inside the envelope. It was obvious that Gopal had loads of news. Atiya sat down to have a good read.

'Dear Atiya,' Gopal wrote. 'I have so much to tell! Sorry for not writing earlier . . .' He went on to give almost a blow-by-blow account of his entire vacation in Chennai. He described his summer physics and chemistry classes—'a ghastly bore!'—and his motorbike driving lesson, 'Just one!' He wrote about his new batch of friends in the school he would soon be joining for his tenth class and the opportunities he would now have, thanks to his father's ambitions for him. 'But Dad also knows what I want to do. He's got in touch with the best wildlife and forestry colleges in the country.' Gopal wrote about his dream of joining the Wildlife Institute in Dehradun and studying wildlife management. 'It is a two year course and I'll get plenty of opportunities to take up projects that'll be interesting for at least ten years!' he wrote, 'I'm determined to go for it, as soon as I complete my B.Sc in Chennai. Just four years from now!' Atiya was thrilled for him. 'And of course,' the letter went on, 'every summer, I'll be coming to see you and your father. I look forward to many more treks in the sanctuary with you both!'

At least he knew what he wanted to do, he was lucky! She, for one, hadn't a clue as yet. She groaned. Things were still so uncertain, at least about her future. What should she study? And where? Should she take up botany in college and go for a forest management course, like her father had suggested? Conversations with Ogre Uncle about the Kurumba tribals were so interesting—perhaps she should do anthropology? Ogre Uncle made his experiences come alive each time he talked about his research work! Or—and this was a tiny half acknowledged thought—should she study music instead? Life was too confusing. Other than Dips, Uncle Dara and Mrs Pillai, there wasn't anyone she could ask for objective advice.

The first three months of school whizzed by much too fast. Atiya was caught in a whirl of tests, revisions, reports, exam sheets and mark sheets, hints and guides. There wasn't much time to think about anything besides books.

However her flute lessons continued and she was glad for that. She would get into the first bus, as soon as Papa drove out of the gate on Saturday mornings. Flute classes with her Ogre Uncle were finally getting somewhere. Even Mishora had begun to notice the improvement in her playing. 'That was delightful!' Mishora praised her after one Saturday lesson, 'You're playing better and better all the time.'

'Yes!' added Ogre Uncle, who quite enjoyed his new name. 'From now on, we are going to play more advanced music. Good work, Atiya, my child!' Atiya put her flute down and gave the old man a hug. She and Mishora had noticed that he was looking thinner lately. He ate less too. 'I don't need that much food!' he would tell them, a little irritated with their pleading. But his moody comments and his irritability were short-lived, and on some days' non-existent. Atiya was glad to notice that Mishora was beginning to look more cheerful and less harassed. The tiny cottage began to ring with laughter and chuckles. Atiya would sometimes stand outside the door and eavesdrop, savouring these moments. She, like Mishora, had no idea how much longer any of this would last. Everyday was a bonus for them.

September onwards, classes became hectic. Exams, teachers kept reminding their students, were around the corner. 'Keep your mind on your studies,' they would often warn the girls and boys. Most, like Atiya, were ambitious, and had their eyes trained on their long term goals. Concentration was a must! No one had time for silly teasing, practical jokes or pranks on their classmates. Atiya was left to her own devices. It was now mid-September and they had five months left for the final exams. The days were beginning to blur into one another, there were massive amount of work to do and lessons to revise.

Atiya felt very guilty when she took the bus each Saturday to the Shivan cottage. Papa had watched her pack her backpack with snacks one Saturday morning with a quizzical expression on his face. If he was suspicious, he didn't say so. Angasammy, who was aware that she caught the bus and went somewhere each weekend with a packed lunch, had not told Papa anything. Her father hadn't the faintest idea of her visits to the Shivan cottage, as she waved him goodbye from the porch. Somehow, she never picked up enough courage to tell him. After a while she gave up. She would wait till the right moment. And so far, the right moment hadn't come.

On one such Saturday, Atiya got onto the usual bus for her lesson with Ogre Uncle. It poured with rain, the monsoons hadn't quite given up and already people were talking of the north east monsoons that were about to begin. She was sick of the wet and muddy roads, her foot often skidded on gravelly bits and she had taken a toss a couple of times. However, Saturdays were special, and nothing could dampen her spirits. She loved her lessons dearly. Mishora and Ogre Uncle always gave her an enthusiastic and warm welcome. A steaming hot cup of cocoa would be pushed into her hands and soon after that, warm on the inside, Atiya and Ogre Uncle would begin their flute lesson for the week.

Now that the trees dripped oodles of rain onto them, they had to move indoors and the cottage echoed with their music. Mishora hummed the tunes they played as she worked in the house. On one occasion, when they played a lively tribal song, she left her kitchen and barefoot, she danced in the tiny sitting room, her hands waving like tree branches in a gentle breeze, her head bending this way and that and her body swaying to the rhythm of the melody. She sang words in her mother tongue as she stepped to the left, then to the right. Atiya watched as she played the duet with Ogre Uncle, not missing a note or a beat and when the final notes came to a sudden and abrupt halt, Mishora and Atiya clapped their hands in a burst of glorious joy. Ogre Uncle let out a lung-swelling, joyous laugh. Atiya stood stock still. This, finally, was her reward—the sound of his happy, uninhibited laughter. After all the months of striving, practise, listening and learning, she had finally been given a beautiful gift. She hugged him tight. 'Oh, Ogre Uncle,' Atiya whispered in his ear with impetuous enthusiasm. 'Thank you, thank you so much!'

The old man was suddenly overcome with emotion and quickly pulled out his handkerchief to blow his nose loudly, trying to make a comedy of the moment. Little did they know it, but he too had suddenly realized how much this girl and the flute lessons had done for him, both mentally and physically! Even though his muscles and his legs became weaker and weaker, his self-awareness had grown ever stronger. He seemed to have earned his self respect again. He woke each morning, with a renewed mission—to be caring and loving to Mishora, who took such selfless care of him and to teach Atiya everything he knew about the flute and as much tribal music as he could. He knew she had the makings of a great musician and the clarity of thought of a true researcher. She had already shown a keen interest in anthropology. A secret desire began to work its way into his subconscious mind. Her two talents might, together, give her the capacity to carry on his great work. He must continue with her lessons as long as he could!

As the pattern of the monsoons changed from the south west to the north east, the days grew colder and shorter. Atiya seemed to need more and more time for her studies. She missed two Saturday lessons, in late December and when she went again, in the first week of January, Mishora opened the front door with tears in her eyes. She gave Atiya an absent-minded hug and silently pulled her in, a finger on her lips. Atiya knew at once, that something had happened to Ogre Uncle.

'What is it?' she asked, the words sticking in her throat. 'Where's Uncle?' Mishora looked distraught. Her hair was untidy, her clothes full of crumples, as if she hadn't had time to dress properly this morning.

'Papa is sick today,' she told Atiya, 'I tried to get him out of bed, but he says he cannot. He feels very weak . . .'

They walked together to his bedroom, where Ogre Uncle lay in a large carved wooden bed. His face looked haggard and he had dark circles under his eyes. He looked ill, his eyes sunken and his wrinkled face—fragile and worn. Atiya's heart sank. She hobbled up to his bed, her shoes scraping on the floor as she came closer to him.

'Good morning, Ogre Uncle!' Atiya tried to hide her anxiety from her voice. Her knees felt weak and wobbly. 'What's up today?' she asked, pretending to be chirpy.

The old man opened his eyes, and looked dimly in her direction. He tried to raise himself on an elbow, but couldn't hold himself up too long. Mishora fussed in the background, fluffing up a pillow here, straightening a blanket there and tidying up things on the dresser.

Ogre Uncle smiled weakly. 'You haven't come f . . .

for two whole weeks! Have you forgotten us . . . and the flute?' he asked trying to smile. He reached out with one hand. Atiya held it in both of hers.

'How could I ever do that? You have taught me so much!' She replied, gently caressing his hand. He looked so ill. 'Have you eaten your breakfast? I'm hungry!' She turned to Mishora, who was already coming in with the steaming cup of hot cocoa. 'Will you eat something with me?' She asked Ogre uncle.

He shook his head, scrunching up his eyes. For the first time, she realized, she was seeing him without his dark glasses on. His eyes, dark brown like her cup of cocoa, were blank. He couldn't see her and his eyes were focussed on one spot, perhaps where a bit of white light made it seem brighter to him. A feeling of utter sadness filled her heart and her chest was tight with sorrow. Her beloved Ogre Uncle had little time left and she worried that he may never get up from his bed again.

She walked to his bedroom window and looked out, trying desperately to compose herself before she faced the old man and Mishora again. Outside, the rain had stopped and a weak sun peeked through the clouds above the opposite riverbank. A movement caught her eye.

It was Rangappa. That was no surprise!

Ever since that first time, when he had appeared suddenly and Atiya had made a comparison between him and Ogre Uncle, the elephant had been turning up on the riverbank every morning. On Saturdays, as usual, he would appear and stand very still, as if he was listening for something. Gently, he pulled up tufts of grass and stuffed them with a twist of his trunk, into his mouth. He chewed calmly, not in a fit of fury and seemed to take time to enjoy what he ate. Mishora watched him one sunny Saturday morning as he walked purposefully up to the edge of the riverbank. He waved his trunk towards them, sniffing the air for their human scent. His ears flapped gently.

'I think,' Mishora said, looking at the animal on the other bank, 'I think he's waiting for something, listening quietly . . .'

When Atiya finally arrived and the lesson began, the animal stood as still as a huge boulder, trunk lying curled upwards, and ears faced forward. He looked like a gentle, grey, giant cuddly toy, harmless and not menacing at all! They stared at him—awestruck. Could the huge old beast actually be listening to the sound of their flutes? Was he enjoying every note they played? Could he be appearing each day for that purpose?

From that day on, lessons never began without both

Atiya and Ogre Uncle wishing the elephant a cheery 'Hello, Rangappa! How are you this morning?' The animal would listen patiently for as long as it took for their lesson. At the end of lesson time, Rangappa would go quietly back into the forest. 'It's as if his lesson,' Atiya would tell Ogre Uncle with a laugh, 'is over too!'

Over the last few weeks, with the excessive rain and with flute lessons conducted indoors, they thought the animal would stop coming. But that was not so. Everyday, there he was, at the proper time, till Saturday came around. He had come for his weekly concert! Ogre Uncle loved it and began to talk to him across the riverbank, whenever Mishora told him that Rangappa was there. She would open the window and call Ogre Uncle to her side.

'Bad weather today!' Uncle would shout across conversationally to the elephant. 'Now don't you get too wet, old chap! You make sure you stay warm. Look after yourself, old man!' Rangappa would snort with his long trunk extended as far out as he could, almost as if he wanted to touch the old man like a friend. Mishora and Atiya loved the exchanges between these two earth creatures—one who couldn't see, the other who couldn't speak. They had finally learnt to communicate better than many who were more fortunate!

Atiya and Mishora spent this morning however, reading to Ogre Uncle while he lay in his bed. Rangappa stood peacefully, on the other bank, for at least two hours. As she was about to leave, the old man suddenly asked Atiya to take a sheet of music he had written out years ago. He pointed at the top of his dresser. Atiya walked to it. On top of a pile of music lay a yellowed piece of paper. It was a composition he said he had heard the Kurumba tribals often play to celebrate great events.

'It's usually played on important occasions,' Ogre Uncle told her, between short, difficult breaths, 'but I haven't played it for years. It's a difficult piece . . . quick notes, lots of sharps and flats . . . and a couple of long, held notes. You'll . . . need to practise it . . . Take your flute home with you, this time.'

Mishora had already wrapped it up and when Atiya said goodbye to the old man and came to the door, she gave the parcelled flute to her. 'Read through that music carefully, Atiya!' she advised. 'It's difficult and will take you time to play well. Go! I hear the bus. Hurry or you'll miss it!' They gave each other a quick hug. Atiya left.

As she sat in the bus, feeling awful about Ogre Uncle's failing health, she felt the flute in the wrapped up paper. How was she going to hide this from her father? And when could she practise at home? It could only be when Papa was out and until just before he returned home.

She might have to make Maniar and Angasammy promise not to tell Papa her secret for a while. As the bus bumped along on the mud road, Atiya vowed she'd get the piece of music note perfect before her next lesson and play it for Ogre Uncle the following Saturday. She was sure that would cheer him up.

PREMONITION

The following week was awful.

Papa would leave the house after she left for school, and return just half an hour after she herself got home. It was almost as if he had sensed her secret. Was he deliberately trying to put a stop to her practice? He had never brought up the subject of flute lessons ever since she had asked him about it ages ago. She was sure he hoped she'd forget about it in a while and that would be that.

A whole week went by, with little or no practice. On Friday morning, Papa told her the Chief Conservator was on a visit to the sanctuary and would be having lunch with them the following day. That of course, was the end of her planned visit to the Shivans for her Saturday lesson.

Frustrated, she met Mrs Pillai on Friday after school, with a sealed envelope in her hands. Inside was a letter Atiya had written in a hurry.

'Please, Mrs Pillai,' she pleaded, 'Would you do me a favour?'

Mrs Pillai was her usual friendly self, 'Yes, tell me, Atiya?'

Atiya gave her the letter. 'Do you know the old gentleman who lives with his daughter, down the road in the last tiled cottage like yourself?'

Mrs Pillai looked blank for a moment and then light dawned on her. She raised her eyebrows. 'You know the Shivans?'

Atiya nodded quickly. She didn't want to explain too much. 'I . . . could you please give his daughter—she's called Mishora—this letter for me?'

Mrs Pillai read the writing on the envelope. 'Mishora and Ogre Uncle' it said in Atiya's neat, clear handwriting. She looked again at Atiya, but the girl was not going to say more. She sensed it. Instead, Mrs Pillai nodded, smiled and said, 'Of course, my dear! Anything else you want me to tell them?'

Atiya would have loved to say a lot more, but she shook her head, and smiled by way of explanation.

'Alright, alright!' Mrs Pillai replied again, laughing tolerantly at her. 'No more questions!'

'Thanks. I . . .I'll tell you later, Mrs Pillai!' Atiya said, looking solemn again. Then she turned quickly on her heel and walked away. She did not want to make a blunder.

The teacher looked after her for a moment, as she put the letter in her bag with her books. She could hear the bus. It was time to go home.

Atiya walked slowly down the road towards the lodge. It was going to be a long, quiet and lonely weekend. Thanks to Mrs Pillai, the letter would explain her inability to attend her Saturday lesson with Ogre Uncle. She hoped he and Mishora would understand. Sardare had already finished his work for the day and drove up behind her, just as she got to the gate. 'Hi!' he said, cheerfully 'Jump in!'

Dhola and Maniar greeted them, as they came up the porch, much as usual. Angasammy brought in tea and biscuits and they relished the warm liquid going down their parched dry throats. 'So,' said Papa. 'What have you been up to?'

Atiya jumped and her bag fell with a crash to the ground. Oh, dear! Had he discovered what she'd been doing, all these Saturdays, she thought, looking terrified. Quickly, and to hide her fear, she bent to pick up her bag and books.

'Nothing much.' She replied, but he was looking at her too sharply. 'I think I'm dead, now!' she thought to herself.

But Papa was only laughing at her. Strange! He'd been in a remarkably good mood lately.

'There's a flute in your room, I see,' she heard Papa say with a smile on his lips. 'Where'd you get that?'

'Uh, from a friend, Papa,' Atiya replied. 'I'm waiting for a teacher to turn up here. Studies, books, tests, revision—at the moment that's all that's on my head!' Atiya managed to get out of her dry mouth. 'Why do you ask?'

To Atiya's relief, Papa laughed again. Gosh, he really had cheered up so much in this last week! He flung his peaked cap in one corner, yanked off his boots, flung them under the sofa and stretched his toes, looking at them as if they weren't his. Atiya wasn't used to this behaviour. She looked at him sharply too.

'What have you been up to, Papa?' she asked him, now. Papa looked mighty relaxed and comfortable. And yet, a little sheepish.

'We . . .ll!' he said, hesitantly. 'I . . .that teacher of yours . . . what's her name . . .er . . .Mrs Pillai! Nice woman.' He said, smiling appreciatively.

'Yes . . .?' Atiya replied, her voice an enquiring drawl.

Papa was grinning from ear to ear now. 'I met her last week, you know, as she was leaving class. We talked a long time. I took her out for a plate of pakodas to that Greens Café, near the Education centre. Well, We have been meeting at lunch time all this week. We talked quite a bit.'

Where was this heading, Atiya wondered? She did recall that he had mentioned he had a crush on her when they were both in college, as teenagers. 'That's nice, Papa, I like Mrs Pillai. She seems like a friendly person.'

Papa was looking pensive suddenly. Then he perked up, and grinned again, 'She thinks you've grown up a lot this term. She tells me you've changed. I'm going to meet her on Sunday morning. She's called me over for a cup of coffee. Want to come?'

'No, but I wish I could, Papa,' Atiya told him. Had Naina Pillai seen her at the Shivans cottage and told Papa so? Now that Atiya had given her the letter, it was obvious that she knew the Shivans. If Naina hadn't told him yet, would she tell him when they did meet on Sunday? 'I've got tests on Monday, and I also have to practise!' Oops, what had she just said?

'Practise what?' asked her father quizzically. He stared at her.

'Nothing, just some chemistry formulas and stuff, that's all!' she said quickly. Just missed being caught! She got up and left the room, breathing a sigh of relief. Papa hadn't realized a thing!

As soon as he left for the Pillai cottage that Sunday, she took out her flute. Maniar and Angasammy were both in the kitchen. She shut her windows and began to practise. First, she took out the yellowed music sheet. The notes and letters had been beautifully written, she recognized the writing. A much younger Ogre Uncle had written them himself. She marvelled at his neat handwriting. It looked as if it had been printed. On the top left hand corner someone had written a date: 7 Dec, 1989, Thengamallai. He had given it a title. 'Happy Spirit' he had written on the top in a neat and precise writing.

The entire piece was in E minor and initially it sounded morose and rather sad. All minor scales are on the melancholy side, she reminded herself. She read through the notes, bar by bar, slowly and carefully. Then picking up her flute, she played the notes, again, very slowly, making sure she played them right. The flats in the piece were difficult to play—there were some tough gaps and jumps. She worked at it till all the notes were correct. The last ten bars of music were composed in a different tempo—slower, romantic and slightly melancholy. It was a very unusual piece—almost as if it described a life story. Gradually, very gradually, she began to play the piece with firm, quick and light fingers, finally achieving the fast tempo of the first portion, then the slower tempo of the last bars, just as was written on the top of the sheet. She practised for at least two hours. It was a great melody, nostalgic and with some quick quavers—fast and furious. Atiya found it impossible to put down the flute till she had mastered it. It was a truly inspiring piece. She loved it!

When Papa finally came roaring up the drive in his

jeep, it was lunchtime. Jumping out of the vehicle from the other side was Mrs Pillai herself. Atiya whooped with delight. He obviously enjoyed Naina Pillai's company. She was glad for him. He had been so lost without her mother for so many years.

'Hi, Mrs Pillai!' she greeted her, 'Nice surprise!'

Naina laughed, dusting her trousers and straightening her shirt, 'I thought you'd say that! I wish Gopal was here too, but the silly boy hasn't even written for two weeks. He's freaking out on the cricket matches, I guess.'

Angasammy brought their Sunday lunch out onto the lawn, under the tree where the garden benches stood. He laid out his typical weekend spread. It was quite a feast and they tucked in happily.

Atiya, Papa and Naina chatted non-stop. Papa, his usual charming self, regaled them with crazy jungle stories. The sun peeked out between the trees. The last two days had been warmer than usual. The birds were out in large mixed parties, foraging in the shrubbery around the edge of the garden. They seemed to be enjoying the warmth of the day too.

Suddenly, they heard a loud fierce trumpeting! Elephant! Papa jumped up and stood still, looking in the direction of the thick forest, at the far end of the garden.

The trumpet had come from there. They heard a couple of twigs breaking, then calmly, majestically, a large male elephant came out to the edge of the forest. He waved his trunk in their direction.

It was Rangappa! Atiya looked at him, a little dazed. What was he doing here? He didn't seem upset, or angry. Ram Sardare was puzzled. He had been told that Rangappa had been behaving oddly docile, as if he had decided he had had enough of his own past behaviour and was trying to turn over a new leaf. But this sudden appearance, so close to human habitation was strange indeed. Something must be wrong with the animal.

'I haven't seen him for weeks!' Papa said in a low whisper. 'The rangers have been telling me about him, though. They say he is less aggressive lately. Wonder why.' He didn't take his eyes off the animal as it stood a hundred metres away.

Rangappa was clearly looking in their direction. His trunk continued to wave about, was he sniffing the air? Was he trying to smell something? Or was he looking for something? Or someone . . . ?

Atiya gasped and clamped her mouth shut suddenly. She had a strange, odd feeling that the beast was looking for *her*. Could that really be the case? And if so, why? Her heart skipped a beat. Was he coming to tell her something? Papa, she could see, was watching him silently, waiting for him to make the first move. Rangappa, however, just stood there, breathing through his trunk, which he waved from time to time, smelling the air and continuing to look in their direction. Finally his ears stopped flapping, his trunk hung limp. He waited. Atiya looked again at the animal and suddenly, she froze. Was it a premonition? She realized it had to be about Ogre Uncle.

She took three quick steps forward, quite forgetting that Papa and Naina were looking at her in surprise. She cupped her hands around her mouth. 'Hello, Rangappa!' Atiya called out calmly to him. It was the usual tone of voice she and the Shivans had used in the jungle, when they spoke to him each time he appeared on the riverbank, on Saturdays. 'What is it? Are you telling me something? What is it?' She was talking to him like a friend, as if she knew him very well indeed.

Papa's mouth dropped in awe. Since when had his daughter begun talking to animals? He couldn't get himself to break this awesome moment between child and animal. It was like an electric current that connected these two. Rangappa stood very still, listening to her calm, quiet words. Did he recognize her voice? And if so, how was that possible? How was it that he, Ram Sardare, hadn't noticed this special ability in his child.

In what crazy disconnected world had he been living? Perhaps this was what Naina had been eluding to—for days. He hadn't an inkling of what was going on in his daughter's life!

Atiya had stopped calling out to the beast. She just stood there, arms down, shoulders drooping, and her head bent to hide her tears. It must be Ogre Uncle! Rangappa, like so many animals, had a sixth sense and had come to tell her that their friend was either very sick or gone forever. She must hurry! She had to go to Mishora! But how? Atiya turned quickly, her eyes still wet with tears. The premonition wouldn't go away. She must help Ogre Uncle, she must get away!

'I'm going to study, Papa,' she told her father, not looking up. Sardare looked stunned, and speechless. He took a step towards her, but Mrs Pillai held up a quick hand, motioning him to let her go. Naina sensed the girl's actions spoke of a profound sorrow and a longing to be by herself.

'Let her be,' Naina whispered to Sardare. 'You can ask her later about all this.' They stood, side by side, and watched as Atiya stumbled across the grass and back into the house.

A PASSING

Next morning, Atiya bunked school. She caught the second bus to the tiled village and walked as fast as she could to the Shivans cottage.

No one answered the door bell when she called, but the door was ajar and she walked right in. In the hall, she saw all the furniture had been moved aside. Ogre Uncle lay on the floor, as if asleep, in a resplendent tussar kurta and pyjama, with a bunch of wild flowers in his kurta buttonhole. His eyes were shut and his wrinkles were gone. His brow was smooth and wise and eternal peace seemed to emanate from him, in an ever-widening 'glow'. Atiya's premonition had turned out true. Ogre Uncle had left them forever. Rangappa's visit had been to tell her so.

Mishora sat on her knees at Ogre Uncle's head. She looked fragile, vulnerable and beyond consolation. Atiya went across to her and they hugged in silence. No words were necessary. They would miss the Ogre always. And the flute, now silenced, would never be heard in this little cottage again. It was unthinkable.

Around the room and out in the back garden, several people hung about. They were Kurumbas. Atiya recognized some of them from the villages around the sanctuary. One owned a tea shop in her own village. Thambi's parents were there too. They looked at her, surprised to see her here amidst all their own people. No one said anything. Many placed bunches of wild flowers at Ogre Uncle's feet. They bent and touched him, paying their last respects. The sorrow in the room was palpable. Atiya's heart and head felt like lead. She, like all the Kurumbas here, would always miss him.

As she watched, the men lifted the old man and carried him away for the simple cremation at the riverbank—

Atiya knew she would never get over his passing. She clung to Mishora and they cried silent tears.

Atiya waited till all the Kurumbas had left, returning to their own hamlets dotted around the sanctuary. She begged Mishora to come back with her and stay for a few days in the lodge, but Mishora wouldn't hear of it. 'Papa knew I was happiest here. I know he is with me in spirit. Now I must stay and clear up the house. There are some things that Papa had asked me to do. I'm going to be busy, thankfully for some time. Will you come on the tenth day for the prayers for his soul? Please?'

Atiya hugged Mishora again. They wiped each other's tears and grew serious. Silently, they tidied the old man's room, putting away things tenderly. His favourite books in Braille, his dark glasses, the soft slippers he wore in the house and the rather worn leather shoes he wore out in the garden. The dresser was loaded with memorabilia from his younger days. There were albums and more books, dozens and dozens of notebooks, crammed to the last line with research notes, photographs and scribbles even on the margins. All in his precise neat handwriting. In one drawer, there were stacks of music sheets. Most of them were yellowed pieces of paper, with dates, places, names and other details in the blank columns on the left side. Atiya picked up the top few and glanced through them, her eyes glistening with tears. She looked at the notes, and an idea began to form in her head. It wasn't the right time to think about such things, but the thought just wouldn't go away. It was almost as if Ogre Uncle was standing and whispering it into her ear. She knew she would not be able to ignore it too long. 'Later!' she promised herself.

Mishora watched her, but didn't say a word. She wondered how Atiya would continue with flute lessons, now that her dear Papa was gone.

Finally, with some of the initial tidying done, Atiya bade Mishora goodbye. Both of them knew they had unfinished things to complete for Ogre Uncle. Now it was time to fulfil the promises they had made to him.

PAPA GETS SUSPICIOUS

Sardare returned home, as usual, quite early. Thank goodness, Atiya had got in just half an hour earlier than he did. Papa seemed pensive. They ate their dinner in silence—each in their own thoughts. When the dessert was over, Papa put down his napkin and cleared his throat.

'How are your studies going, Atiya?' he asked, his brows furrowed. She was certain he was definitely distracted, with thoughts other than work.

Atiya shrugged. 'Okay, I guess,' she replied. 'Biology, chemistry and physics are cool. But Maths is my big bugbear! I just hope I pass, that's all!'

Papa smiled. 'Naina tells me you're doing fine.' He gave her a sharp look. 'The other day she told me you may have something to tell me?' Had Naina told him about the letter she had sent to the Shivans?

He recalled his daughter's conversation with Rangappa, and a few hints that Naina had given him when they last met. He was thinking of the flute in her room and a conversation he had overheard in the village.

Atiya jumped. What was Papa implying? She swallowed, not looking at him directly, till she gathered enough courage to do so. 'Not really, Papa,' she told him, 'What does she mean?'

'Don't ask me,' retorted Papa shortly, 'Maybe we need to have a talk about that someday?'

Atiya noticed that Papa was still looking sharply at her—he obviously hadn't believed a word she had said. What had Naina Pillai told him? Had she found out that Atiya had been visiting the Shivans all summer? Atiya had asked her to pass on that letter to Mishora, hadn't she? Had she heard her flute lessons in the tiled cottage, not so distant from her own?

Perhaps Mishora had let the cat out of the bag by mistake. Atiya had the unnerving feeling that Naina knew more about Atiya than she had let on, and was probably trying to tell her father in as tactful a manner, so that Sardare wouldn't hit the roof, when he did get to know of it at some point!

Atiya knew now, that she would have to tell her father soon. Sadly, today didn't seem the right day. She was terrified she would break down completely when she told her father about Ogre Uncle and the wonderful lessons she had had with the old man. Now that her dear Ogre Uncle was gone, the sorrow of his passing would remain for a long, long time. How was she going to be calm and tearless through the telling of her story? She sighed, afraid to speak. It would just have to wait till next weekend. The last thing she wanted was for Papa to put a stop to her visits to the Shivans cottage. Not for another ten days. She still had one more promise to keep for Ogre Uncle. She decided she would tell Papa everything after the tenth day ceremony was over and she was home.

The week went by at a snail's pace. The guilt weighed heavy on Atiya's mind and she tried to avoid Papa during their meals. She evaded his questions by asking him about his own work. His stories were always so interesting, often quite funny. Lately he'd been talking a lot about Rangappa, the rogue elephant.

'The rangers cannot believe that the guy is the same elephant!' he told her one evening. Winter nights were cold and often wet. Manniar would light a fire in the fireplace and father and daughter would warm their toes next to the grate, along with Dhola. The dog loved the warmth, completely unafraid of the fire and would crawl closer and closer, almost into the fireplace, as the embers burnt down to ashes. Atiya and Papa often wondered how he got away unscathed, each time. Surely by now his coat should have been a clump of burnt up fur.

'Rangappa has changed, in a strange way.' Papa was telling her, a little perplexed. 'He doesn't seem half as fierce as before, which is most unusual. The rangers do not see him with a herd, so he is still on his own, but he doesn't enter the surrounding farms and sugar cane fields any more. He seems to have found a space, deep in the jungle where he can stay away from human beings. Two of the older Kurumbas who inhabit the other side of the sanctuary tell me the animal is often spotted on the riverbank, close to the iron bridge, opposite the tiled cottages. Wonder what he finds there?'

Atiya bent quickly to throw a log into the fire. She didn't want Papa to see her red face. If he asked her, she would have to tell him why. She watched the tiny red sparks fly as she raked the embers together, smiling as Dhola decided it was time to creep a bit closer to the warmth.

'Crazy dog!' she said ruffling his neck.

Papa stood up, pulling his chair back to its original place. 'Well, I better get on with the paperwork. And you, young lady, better get cracking with your tests, I suppose!'

It was nearly February, the Board exams were due in just a month's time. April was round the corner. She thought of Gopal. She had recently had another letter from him. She must write to him, too. Atiya wished her father good night and went to her room. Thankful that for another day, at least, her secret was still her own. There were just three days to go. She would tell Papa everything after she had attended Ogre Uncle's prayer ceremony. She was guilty and was prepared to take Papa's fury and punishment.

But first, somehow, she had to thank Ogre Uncle for everything he had taught her. And nothing, not even her father, was going to prevent her from doing that.

FAREWELL

The tenth day was soon upon them. As it was a Saturday, Atiya stayed in her room till the last moment.

Angasammy greeted her with his usual cheery 'Good morning, Atiya Missy!' and placed the breakfast eggs and toast in front of her. Quickly she gobbled it up. 'Where is Papa?' she asked him.

'Dorai had to go for a meeting,' he told her. 'He will not be back for lunch.'

'Oh, I see,' Atiya replied quietly, thinking of her own plans. 'I don't think I will come home on time, either. Don't make lunch for us, please?'

Angasammy looked calm and placid. He didn't think it was his business to ask where she was going. 'When you coming home?' was all he asked her.

'I'll be late, Angu,' she told him, 'But, don't worry. I'll be back as soon as possible!' She knew that depended on how the day at Mishora's would go. Perhaps she may want help with something. Atiya realized that it may be the last time she would meet Mishora in many months. There were the exams to think about too. And who knew what Mishora's plans were . . .

Taking her raincoat and the usual water bottle in a sling bag, she walked down the road and caught the bus. Saturday was market day and the village was packed with people. A good day for poachers to be left to their own devices, she thought. Papa must have got wind of a poaching gang out to make a 'killing' and gone off with his rangers to ambush them. Atiya was a little surprised that he hadn't told her anything this morning before he left. Perhaps he thought she was still asleep, or that she was studying. At least she was spared of having to tell him where she herself was headed. Atiya had already decided that tonight at dinner, she would spill the beans. Not just about the flute lessons and her long wonderful association with the Shivans, but the treks in the sanctuary and the incidents with Rangappa. She had spent these last ten sleepless nights working out her own future plans and today, as she jolted around in the bus along the potholed tracks, everything had suddenly all come together and made a whole lot of sense. She hoped that tonight as she told her father he would understand.

As she walked from the last bus stop to the Shivans cottage, she saw a long line of people walking along in front of her. They were Kurumbas from every tiny hamlet dotting the sanctuary edges. They came from Thengamallai and Innur, from her own village to Badlanganna, from the North to the South and from the East to the West of the Sanctuary borders—men, women and children. They were dressed in their best clothes and they walked along quietly.

Mishora stood at the front door, welcoming all of them with her usual warmth. She gave Atiya a hug, like she did with many of the other women who walked into the cottage before and after her. Today, Atiya noticed, she looked fresh and her eyes were shining again. She had tucked three freshly carved bamboo sticks into her hair which was tied in a knot at the nape of her neck. She wore a plain cream tussar lungi, with a simple green and red border and a green blouse to match. And as usual, she was barefoot.

Mishora waved them all through to the back garden, where several rugs of all colours had been placed on the grass. A single empty armchair faced the visitors. Atiya recognized it at once. It was Ogre Uncle's. On the seat, and framed in simple wood, was a lovely picture of the old man, smiling, eyes crinkled up in joy. A small clay diya was placed on a stone in front of the picture, its cotton wick lit and braving the breeze—there was plenty that morning. Its tiny flame glowed and shone down on everyone seated on the rugs, as if Ogre Uncle's warmth and affection for these Kurumbas was reflected in its glow. Several young Kurumba children placed wild flowers around the picture. The prayer session began.

A Kurumba elder lit a small packet of sandalwood incense sticks, and in a sing-song voice, low but clear, he began to talk to Ogre Uncle.

'We have come to see you one last time, Shivan Dorai,' said the old white-haired man. 'It was God's blessings that gave you to us! We had good times with you and we want you to have good times now in your new abode. God go with you!' Several seated Kurumbas mumbled 'Yes, yes!' agreeing with the first speaker.

Others, like the old Kurumba, came forward to 'talk' to Ogre Uncle, each in some way describing his or her relationship with him. Atiya had never seen a service like this one. No prayers, no rituals, no incantations, no meaningless, endless chanting. It was as if Ogre Uncle, in some strange way, was still with them, for just a while more, and they wanted him to go in peace, because they would not be able to see or speak to him again. No one wept. There was an undercurrent of joy and peace here within this gathering. Atiya felt it strongly and deeply.

When the last old Kurumba's words faded away and the group was getting restless, Atiya knew her moment with Ogre Uncle had come. Quick as lightning she picked up her backpack and opened up the top. Inside, her bamboo flute lay wrapped in a thin cloth.

Atiya took out the flute and walked to Ogre Uncle's armchair. Facing the picture and with her back to the rest of the gathering, she lifted the flute to her lips and blew gently into it. The Kurumbas heard that first note and a hush fell over them. As if under a spell, they sat and listened to her play 'The Happy Spirit'. It was the piece that Ogre Uncle had given to her three weeks earlier. She had practised it over and over for more than a week. Mishora recognized it at once. Many of the older Kurumbas recognized it too. Atiya played it as if she was in a dream. And for the Kurumbas and even Mishora, it was as if Ogre Uncle was back with them for a few more precious minutes.

The notes crept slowly, first, over the group gathered on the forest grass. Gradually the music built up in tempo till it reached a furious, frenetic pace. The music was energetic, yet positive. There was even an answering melody that could just be heard beneath the more prominent one. This one was lower in pitch and more melancholy. As she played on, the others saw a movement on the other bank. Atiya didn't even have to look. She knew it was Rangappa, also come to pay his last respects to dear Ogre Uncle! As was his usual custom, he just stood there, facing them, his ears flapping ever so gently and his trunk raised, almost in silent salute. The Kurumbas gasped in surprise, but the music carried on, unstoppable. Finally with a deep breath, she played the last part of the piece, slowing down to the rhythm of the ending. A long, quiet, pensive final note, and then it was over.

Mishora ran across to Atiya and they hugged, the tears silently pouring down their cheeks, the sorrow too much to contain. They wept, oblivious of the others around them.

'Thank you, thank you!' Mishora whispered between her tears. 'Do you know that Papa played the same piece when Mama died? It was my father's favourite piece. You played it exactly as he would have wished! Papa must be so happy. Oh, Atiya! It's the best tribute you could have made to him.' They hugged again.

A very old Kurumba stood up, watching the elephant. When the music died away, he pointed at the animal. 'Aaaiyee! See Ayyappa?' he said loudly. Everyone stopped to look at the elephant. 'That's old Rangappa!'

'Aaiyee!' the gathered Kurumbas nodded in agreement.

'Rangappa's mahout was also a flute player,' said the wise old man. He must have been at least seventy-five-years-old and not a local Kurumba.

'When his young mahout died suddenly,' he told the rest, 'Rangappa never got over his sorrow. He just became more and more bad-tempered and no one could control him any more. Finally, they had to banish him back into the sanctuary.'

Suddenly, Atiya heard a familiar voice. A male voice she knew only too well. 'So *that's* the reason for his bad behaviour!' It was Papa. 'I wish we'd known about that when I was first posted here years ago. No wonder he has calmed down in the past few months. It's the flute he hears again, after all these years!'

Papa stood at the back and looked directly at his daughter. 'That was beautiful!' He was wearing his white khadi kurta pyjama. He had come to attend the tenth day ceremony, too. How long had he been there?

When did he come in? Had he seen her earlier? Why had he not said anything to her, she wondered? He wasn't after poachers after all. Her mind was a whirl! Mishora smiled calmly at the two of them. Then she turned away gracefully to thank the other visitors, leaving father and daughter to each other.

Atiya swallowed in terrified silence. She waited for Papa's wrath to descend on her, but Papa was as quiet as a mouse. He just looked at her, the gentlest of smiles on his face, even pride, Atiya thought. He had never wanted her to learn to play any musical instrument and here he was, just smiling benevolently at his almost grown up daughter. She couldn't understand it at all.

'Papa?' she said under her breath.

Papa was rubbing the back of his own neck. 'Your music gave me goosebumps, it was so good!' he said in quiet, surprised admiration as he walked up to her. 'I need not ask where you learnt to play like that!'

Atiya was caught off guard. Here was Papa demanding answers. She did want to tell him everything, especially as she now realized that he wasn't mad at her any more. But duty called. Mishora was saying goodbye to all their Kurumba people. She must go to her too.

'We shall wait, Ram,' said another voice, as if reprimanding him, for his demands on his daughter. 'Can't you see she is busy?' It was Naina Pillai, who was standing in a pale yellow sari, by his side. She smiled at Atiya, pulling him away, as she spoke. 'Look!' she told him, pointing across the bank. 'Look at old Rangappa!'

Atiya saw her father turn away to watch the animal. There was no surprise on his face. The events of the past two hours had shaken him from the depths of his heart. He had learnt so much. And so many questions that had been bothering him for weeks had suddenly been answered. Now, all at once, he knew what Naina Pillai had been implying. Atiya's secret was about learning the flute with none other than his old friend Krish Shivan. Hadn't he known Shivan so many years ago, when he, Ram Sardare had joined the Forest Service and was transferred to this sanctuary the first time? Ram had often been told the man was doing such commendable research work with the Kurumbas of the region. Years later, on a third transfer to this sanctuary, Shivan had become ill and though he knew they had bought a tiny tiled cottage in this village, Ram had never had the time to come and visit Shivan and his daughter. The years had flown by and now, the old man was gone.

The flute? That was an old story. He knew perfectly well that the old man had mastered the instrument and learnt and catalogued all the Kurumba music he could lay his hands on. His work was absolutely fantastic, but in his growing illness, he had obviously not bothered too much about documenting this—at least for the relevant departments. What a pity it would be lost forever!

Or would it?

CATCH THE BREEZE

The Board exams were done. The vacations had begun. Atiya and Papa were on their way to meet Mishora.

'I'll drop you at the Shivan cottage,' he told Atiya, 'and make a quick patrol of the area while you're there.'

The jeep ride was super that morning! The teak canopy was thinning and summer had truly arrived—hot, dry winds, forest fires, visitors and the hullabaloo of their vehicles in the sanctuary. An awful time for all wildlife and for those who cared for the forest.

Papa drove over the iron bridge. The jeep skid over a loose pebble, it flew out from under the wheel, through the iron girders into the river below. Plonk! A couple of alarmed ducks quacked, flapping their wings noisily in their agitation to get off the water and away. The jeep turned right on the other end of the bridge and they passed the tiled cottages, one by one. When they came by the Grandfather Banyan tree, Naina came to her door and waved. 'Hi!' she called out to them. 'Where are you off to?'

'To Mishora!' Atiya cupped her hands and hollered back. 'Want to come?'

Naina shook her head, 'No, I have to catch up with housework!' She smiled and made a face. 'But I have a letter for you from Gopal.'

'Come with me for a drive!' Papa invited with a grin.

'If you can come back and get me in . . .' Naina looked at her watch, 'fifteen minutes, yes, I'll come with you?'

Papa laughed, and he said, 'Okay, I'll do that. Get ready quick!' He revved up and they drove on to the Shivans cottage.

As the road curved, they heard the sound of young children's voices. They came from the last cottage and as they approached, Papa and Atiya saw a dozen young children running about in Mishora's garden. At the end of it, under the familiar arjuna tree, they saw Mishora in her father's armchair, with a book in her lap, reading to a group of six-year-olds. Whatever had happened to the peace and tranquillity at the Shivans cottage? Atiya gasped in shock.

Papa watched his daughter walk as quickly as she could, across the side of the house to the back garden. From his jeep, he could just see Shivan's daughter, still reading from her book, the youngsters at her feet completely absorbed in her story. He watched them laugh, and clap their hands each time Mishora stopped, looking at the children with her eyes open wide in mock drama. Mishora looked angelic today surrounded by these little children. Atiya waited till she had finished. She put away her book. The kids scrambled to their feet and she let them scamper off to play with the others.

'Hi!' Mishora called out to her, 'What's up?'

'I should be asking you that question!' Atiya said, indignantly. They hugged. Mishora was smiling happily. Her hair was all over the place, but she looked fit and happy again. Her apron was covered in flour, 'Oh, I was halfway through the cooking,' she apologized, and stretched to undo the knot at her back. 'Can you guess what I'm doing, then?' she asked Atiya.

Atiya looked a little blank. 'Tell?' she said, grinning broadly. She was relieved to see that Mishora was busy and happy.

Mishora's eyes sparkled with life. She grabbed Atiya, and pulled her indoors through the back door.

Inside, the tiny sitting room had changed. Two rows of small chairs and tables stood one behind the other, with an aisle in between. At one end an important looking blackboard stood on a stand. Next to it a straight backed chair stood behind a table. Someone had written the letters A B C in capitals and drawn some pictures next to the letters. This was a classroom!

Atiya looked again, and jumped for joy. She grabbed Mishora in delight.

'An absolutely super idea!' she whooped. 'What made you think of this?'

Mishora smiled and clapped her hands. 'Papa! Who else?' she said, 'He suggested I open a school for Kurumba children after he passed away.'

'Oh, Mishora!' Atiya exclaimed again. 'Ogre Uncle couldn't have thought of anything better for you It's marvellous!'

Mishora nodded enthusiastically. She told her she already had twenty-one students and from what Atiya noticed, all the children seemed thrilled with their new little forest school!

'Papa left something in a Trust fund for me,' she told Atiya. 'I'm going to use it for my Forest School. There's a lot I can do for the Kurumba children. The advantage is that all the parents here know me too. If things go well, I might even have to advertise for other teachers, to help educate the older ones!'

They drank their glasses of juice out at the end of the garden, while Mishora's little children shrieked and whooped around the two of them. Suddenly a cracking twig made them turn and there, in his usual place, on the opposite riverbank, stood Rangappa!

'He comes everyday!' Mishora said matter-of-factly. 'It's hard to believe, but I think he loves the sound of the children's voices. I haven't heard him trumpet or throw a tantrum even once. I think he's really trying to be good again.'

Atiya gaped, unable to say a word. A sense of déjà vu

gripped her for an instant, but she let it pass. Somehow, she felt a reassuring presence close by, watching over them, smiling and glad that things had turned out the way they did. Atiya knew it could only be the happy spirit of dear old Ogre Uncle. They finished their juice, talking animatedly about Atiya's future plans.

'I'm going to take up anthropology.' Atiya told her, excitedly. 'Papa knows now, and he thinks I'll do fine. I'll stay with my aunt and uncle in Bangalore. I'll return here as soon as possible, to take up where your father left off. I'm going to carry on the research on the Kurumbas of this area, and document all the remaining music. What do you think?'

Mishora gaped, she held her hands to her cheeks, amazed. 'Papa's work?' she asked. 'Atiya, you're not going to believe me. Come with me!' and she grabbed Atiya's arm and dragged her to her father's room. On the dresser, now spotless and dustfree, stood a framed picture of Ogre Uncle and leaning against it was an envelope. ATIYA SARDARE, it said in neat capital letters.

'This is for you!' Mishora told her, giving her the envelope. 'I had to write it for him,' she said quietly. 'Papa dictated it to me, just a day after you were here for your last lesson. Read it, please?'

Inside the envelope was a single sheet of lined paper. In Mishora's flowing writing, Atiya read . . .

'To my dear, diligent and delightful ATIYA, I bequeath all my Kurumba music and my research papers of forty-five years of work. The Kurumbas will have to wait till she completes her studies, but I think the wait will be worthwhile. I am certain that Atiya will return to complete my work in this field and will go on to do wonders for this marvellous community.

The Kurumbas and Atiya Sardare will benefit from this association, for I sense a long term and fulfilling relationship between them, much like the one I have been lucky to have with Atiya and the Kurumbas, too.'

Atiya swallowed hard. How had Ogre Uncle realized her interests long before she herself had, she thought? And was it him, speaking to her from the other world, leading her to this new realization of her own talents? Her eyes misted for a few seconds. Dear old Ogre Uncle! She would never forget him. 'Thank you!' she spoke to him in her head. 'I think your father understood me much more than I understood myself.' Was all she managed to say.

They walked into the brand new classroom, as the children began filing in for the morning's last lesson.

Suddenly, Mishora ran back into the bedroom again. She came out with Ogre Uncle's carved bamboo flute and gave it to Atiya. 'This is for you, Papa told me you must keep it.'

Atiya held it gently in her hands, her mind going tenderly over all the many things Ogre Uncle and she had discussed and achieved these last six months of his life. As the children sat down, she picked up the flute and held it lightly to her lips.

Mishora and the children listened as Atiya began to play. As the notes washed over all of them, the children fell silent. First she played a quiet melody to calm them, leading them into a tranquil, contemplative mood. The notes became stronger and louder as she increased her tempo and then, with swift, lightning and yet light and easy touch she skimmed over the flute, blowing and breathing skilfully as she played. The children sat glued to their seats. They loved it! She charmed them completely. On and on went the music, till, in the final bars, she grew softer, but not decreasing in tempo, till the very last note. As suddenly as she had began, the music was over. An awestruck silence filled the room. Mishora and Atiya exchanged a knowing look. They had heard this piece so often under the arjuna tree.

Abruptly, Atiya packed the flute away and got up. The children looked from her to their teacher and smiled in open admiration. Then they clapped. They whooped for joy, they chuckled with glee and they hammered their desks, asking for more. Mishora put up her hand. They could hear a jeep hooting at the front gate. It was Papa and Naina, returning from his jungle patrol.

Atiya walked to the door and she and Mishora hugged each other goodbye. As she got in the jeep, Mishora called out to her. 'Now you know why you have to come back when your studies are done!'

'I cannot wait!' was all Atiya could say in reply.

She knew there would be a lot to tell Papa, Naina and Gopal, and she knew they would be thrilled for her. As she got into the jeep, she recalled the lyrics of the tribal song she had learnt so many months ago:

> The Breeze blows my song through the ancient Forest,
>
> Hear it, my Friend, oh hear it, then!
>
> Casting a Spell over all of us Creatures . . .
>
> Peace, it says, is a Friend we all can share,
>
> Join hands . . . and . . . catch the Breeze . . .!

Atiya knew she would soon be back to catch that forest breeze.